Who had shot at ...

There was little question in Hannah's mind that the bullet had been meant for her.

Or maybe the bullet had been meant for Nick. Somebody wanted him dead because he dared to defend her. She really had no idea what to believe. All she knew for sure was that chills of fear overtook her. The tears that had burned hot in her eyes now fell down her cheeks.

Nick came back into the shop. "Whoever it was, he or she is probably gone by now. Hey...hey, don't cry," he said softly and then he drew her into his arms and held her. "We're safe and everything is going to be all right. I've got you."

His strong arms embraced her and his scent filled her head.

For just that moment she felt protected and cared for.

He held her for several long moments, his heartbeat strong and steady against her frantic one.

SWAMP SHADOWS

CARLA CASSIDY

Harlequin

INTRIGUE

Harlequin®
INTRIGUE™

Recycling programs for this product may not exist in your area.

ISBN-13: 978-1-335-45738-7

Swamp Shadows

Copyright © 2025 by Carla Bracale

 Harlequin Enterprises ULC
22 Adelaide St. West, 41st Floor
Toronto, Ontario M5H 4E3, Canada
www.Harlequin.com

Printed in Lithuania

MIX
Paper | Supporting responsible forestry
FSC® C021394

Carla Cassidy is an award-winning, *New York Times* bestselling author who has written over 170 books, including 150 for Harlequin. She has won the Centennial Award from Romance Writers of America. Most recently she won the 2019 Write Touch Readers' Award for her Harlequin Intrigue title *Desperate Strangers*. Carla believes the only thing better than curling up with a good book is sitting down at the computer with a good story to write.

CAST OF CHARACTERS

Heather LaCrae—Is she an innocent victim or a cold-blooded killer?

Nick Monroe—Can he keep Heather from going to prison? More important, can he keep her alive when danger comes to call?

Bruno Foret—Is the private investigator working to keep Heather out of prison, or is he secretly sabotaging her case?

Tommy Radcliffe—The prosecuting attorney wants Heather behind bars, and Tommy doesn't like to lose.

Wesley Simone—How many secrets did the dead man have?

Chapter One

Heather LaCrae crawled through the darkness of sleep, seeking the light of full consciousness. She felt as if she'd been asleep for days...weeks even, so deep had her dreamless slumber been.

The first thing she noticed before she even opened her eyes was the strange smell of antiseptic and disinfectant. She frowned. Her shanty didn't smell like this, rather it was fragrant with the scents of all kinds of herbs and flowering plants.

She finally opened her eyes and stared around her. She was in a hospital bed. Had she somehow hurt herself? The last thing she remembered was sitting on a stool at the bar in the Voodoo Lounge. Had she fallen off the high chair and somehow hit her head?

That was the only thing that could explain her lack of memory from the night before. She moved her legs, and they seemed to be okay. She then moved her arms and froze. Her right wrist was handcuffed to the bed's railing.

Panic seared through her as she stared at the metal ring encircling her wrist. She was handcuffed! What on earth was going on? She jerked up to a sitting position and then saw the uniformed officer seated in a chair in the doorway to her hospital room.

"Hello? Uh… Officer?"

The young man got to his feet. "My name is Officer Joel Smith." He offered her no smile.

"Uh… Officer Smith, can you tell me what's going on here?" She tried to tamp down the anxiety that threatened to close off the back of her throat. She didn't know why she appeared to be arrested, but this all had to be some sort of a huge mistake.

"I'll just go get the doctor and the chief. They'll be able to explain everything to you," he said. He stepped out into the hallway, where she heard him put in a call to Chief of Police Etienne Savoie. All Smith said was "She's awake," and then he ended the call.

He then called to somebody down the hall and asked for the doctor. It was obvious he wasn't leaving her alone. What did he think she was going to do? Gnaw through the handcuff and then throw herself out of the nearby window?

"Somebody will be in here to explain things to you soon," he said and then returned to his chair in the doorway.

She felt as if she were in a bad dream, one that she couldn't awaken from. She was no criminal. She'd never been in trouble in her entire life. So, what could she have done that warranted the handcuff and an armed guard at her door? And why…oh why couldn't she remember the events of the night before? Whatever it was that had happened that found her here?

She raised the head of her bed and glanced toward

the window. The sun was setting in the sky. How was that possible? Where had the day gone? Confusion twisted and turned in her mind, adding to the vague headache that had been present since she had first opened her eyes.

About fifteen minutes later, the chief of police of the small town of Crystal Cove, Louisiana, came into her room along with Dr. Dwight Maison. She knew the doctor because he had treated her less than a month ago when she'd fallen ill with a sinus infection. A round of strong antibiotics had fixed her right up, but she had a feeling there was no prescription that was going to fix this situation easily.

She focused on Chief Etienne Savoie. She'd seen him around town before and knew he was considered one of the town's most eligible bachelors. His gray eyes gazed at her soberly. "Ms. LaCrae," he began with a curt nod of his head.

"Please…make it Heather," she replied, her nerves burning so hot inside her she feared she might internally combust. "Can you please tell me what's going on here?"

"Heather LaCrae, you are under arrest for the murder of Wesley Simone."

"What?" She stared at him in utter shock. "Wh-what are you talking about? I didn't murder anyone. I… I could never murder anyone."

"Late last night, you were found in the alley behind the Voodoo Lounge. Wesley was next to you, dead by several stab wounds. You had the knife in your hand,

and you were covered in his blood. There was also a confession in your phone messages."

Heather stared at the dark-haired official in horror. "Is this some kind of a bad joke? This is all a huge mistake," she protested, her voice growing in volume and intensity. "I don't care how I was found, I couldn't kill anyone."

"I need to inform you of your rights," Etienne said, and as he went into the whole spiel, she continued to stare at him in disbelief. She'd had a murder weapon in her hand? A knife? And she'd been covered in Wesley's blood? No way…there was no way in hell she believed she'd stabbed a man—any man—to death.

"What happens now?" she asked once Etienne was finished with the Miranda rights.

"Dr. Maison will check you out and make sure there are no lingering complications from whatever you took to commit suicide last night."

Heather hadn't believed she could be any more stunned, but she'd been wrong. This news finally brought tears of frustration to her eyes. "I would never commit suicide, and I would never, ever stab a man to death."

"Then you want to talk to me about what happened last night at the Voodoo Lounge?" Etienne asked.

How could she tell him what had happened when she didn't know what happened. Her last memory was sitting in the Voodoo Lounge next to Wesley at the bar. She remembered small-talking with the man, and that was it.

"I… I think I'd like a lawyer," she said, realizing the severity of the situation. The tears came faster and faster, chasing each other down her cheeks, one right after another.

She silently cried as Dr. Maison took her blood pressure and then listened to her heart. She continued to weep as he removed the IV line and then pronounced her good to go.

At that point Etienne handed her a brown paper bag that she hadn't even noticed he'd held. "I took the liberty of speaking to Lucy Dupree this afternoon. Somebody told me you are close friends. Anyway, she gathered up some clothes for you to wear out of here since the clothing you had on last night has been taken as evidence. You can go ahead and change now." He unlocked the handcuff that had chained her to the railing.

She slid out of the bed, and on shaky legs she headed to the bathroom. Once there, she managed to get her emotions under control, although she was still in a daze of disbelief. Lucy had apparently gone to her shanty to get the clothes. The two were good enough friends that Lucy had a key to her place and Heather had a key to Lucy's.

She tossed the blue-flowered hospital gown to the floor and then dressed in the panties and bra Lucy had provided. She pulled on the pair of gray jogging pants and the pink T-shirt. There was also a hairbrush, which she was grateful for.

For several minutes, she stood in front of the small mirror over the sink and brushed out her long, dark hair. After that, she remained in front of the mirror, staring at her reflection.

She didn't care how much evidence they had against

her, there was no way she had killed a man who had only been a casual acquaintance to her. But it worried her that she couldn't remember what had happened. How had she gotten into the alley, covered in blood and next to a dead man?

Something evil was at play here. She couldn't help but believe somebody had set her up. She had to have been drugged, and once her body was placed next to Wesley's body, whoever it was had typed a confession into her phone.

It was the only scenario that made a kind of sick sense. But who? Who could have done this to her?

A knock on the door pulled her from her troubling thoughts. "Heather, it's time for us to go," Etienne called through the door.

With a deep breath for strength, Heather opened the door and stepped out of the bathroom. "I'm sorry, but I have to follow protocol," Etienne said as he turned her around and then placed her in handcuffs.

The cold bite of the metal around her wrists made everything even more real. Once again, she was in a daze as Etienne and Officer Smith escorted her out of the room and down the long hallway to the exit.

Darkness had begun to fall outside as they led her to a patrol car and helped her into the back seat. The two men spoke for a minute or two, and then Officer Smith took off walking, and Etienne got into the driver seat of the car she was in.

Once again Heather was in a frightened haze as he started the car and they left the hospital parking lot. Chief Savoie didn't speak to her, and she didn't talk to him. She had nothing to say at this point and was afraid to say anything without a lawyer present.

It didn't take them long to reach the police station. The Crystal Cove Police Department was housed in a large, one-story building painted an attractive turquoise.

Etienne drove around to the back of the building and parked. He helped her out of the back seat and then led her through the back door.

"You are going to be arraigned tomorrow afternoon, so you might want to line up a lawyer before then," he said as they walked down a long hallway. "I'll be glad to provide you with a list of names of public defenders."

They walked into a large room where three jail cells were side-by-side. There were no prisoners at the moment, but the sight of the bars and the bunk beds and open toilets shot a new wave of fear through her. This was serious. Oh God, she was in deep trouble, and she wasn't sure she trusted a public defender to represent her in a murder case.

"Actually, I'd like to call Nick Monroe," she replied. She had never met the man before, didn't even know what he looked like, but she had heard he had represented several people from the swamp in a variety of matters. "Could you get me his number?"

"Absolutely. In fact, I'll take you to a conference room right now so you can have some privacy while you make the call." Instead of putting her into one of the cells, he took her back down the hallway to a small room with a table and four chairs.

"I'll be right back," he said. He was gone only minutes, and then he returned with a cell phone and a phone number written down on a piece of paper. "One call, Heather, and when you are finished just knock on the door." With that, he left and closed the door behind him.

Gingerly, she picked up the phone and turned it on. She went to the phone icon and pulled up the keypad. Her fingers trembled as she punched in Nick Monroe's number.

It rang three times, and then a deep voice answered. "Monroe Law. This is Nick Monroe."

"Mr. Monroe, my name is Heather LaCrae, and I'm in terrible trouble." To her horror, once again she began to cry.

IT TOOK NICK over fifteen minutes to calm the crying woman on the other end of the phone. Finally, she told him why she had called and that she was to be arraigned the next afternoon. He agreed to meet with her the next morning, and from there he would decide if he was going to represent her.

The first thing he did after speaking to her was call Etienne to get the rundown of the case and the evidence found at the scene. It was all definitely damning. He had no idea if Heather LaCrae was guilty or not. He would know more after meeting with her in the morning.

If he did decide to represent her, it would be one of the most serious cases he'd ever worked. He not only represented people from the town of Crystal Cove, but also those who lived in the swamp that half surrounded the small town.

He charged a good fee to the people he knew could

afford it, and he made other arrangements for the people from the swamp who he knew couldn't.

That was his way of giving back. Having been raised in an affluent family and blessed with a large trust fund, Nick had never had to worry about money. However, he knew there were others who didn't have what he had, and those were the ones he tried to help.

He didn't know Heather LaCrae, but Etienne had told Nick that Heather was from the swamp and made a living by selling fresh herbs to the café and the restaurant in town. She also had a little store in town where she sold her herbs, spices, flowers and plants.

Even though she appeared to have a strong work ethic, he suspected there was no way she could ever pay him for his services. So, if he represented her, it would probably be a pro bono case. Still, he was definitely intrigued by the elements of the crime.

The next morning at ten o'clock, he arrived at the jail to meet with his potential client. Etienne met him in the police station lobby. Despite their opposing professions, the two had been good friends for years.

"Good morning, Chief Savoie," he greeted his friend.

"Good morning to you. I'm assuming you're here to meet with your client. I've got to tell you, Nick, if you decide to take this one on, it's definitely going to be an uphill battle for you," Etienne said.

Nick grinned at him. "You know I've always liked a good challenge."

"I don't know, Nick. All I can tell you is the physical evidence is definitely stacked against her," Etienne replied. "I'll take you to the conference room so you can talk to her."

Etienne led him to the small conference room where Nick had met many clients in the past. The chief of police left him to go get Heather, and while Nick cooled his heels, he opened the notebook he'd brought with him and pulled a pen from his shirt pocket.

He was definitely intrigued to see what the woman accused of such a heinous crime looked like. He already knew the physical evidence was damning and she would be facing a murder charge.

He sat up straighter as he heard Etienne approaching the room again. A rivulet of surprise raced through him as Heather LaCrae came into the room.

The first thing that surprised him was her beauty. Her hair fell around her shoulders in a curtain of rich darkness, and her dark eyes were long-lashed. High cheekbones and lush-looking lips added to her overall loveliness.

The second thing that surprised him was the fact that she was a petite, slender woman who, at the moment, looked frail and frightened. She wore a pair of jogging pants and a pink T-shirt that showed off her slim but shapely body.

He immediately got to his feet. "Hi, I'm Nick Monroe, and you must be Heather LaCrae. Please, have a seat." He gestured to the chair across the table from him.

"It's nice to meet you," she said, and once she was seated, Nick sat back down. "I… I seem to be in need of a defense attorney." Tears suddenly appeared in her eyes and clung to her long lashes.

"Well, as luck would have it, I am a defense attorney," he replied lightly, hoping to halt her tears.

"I didn't do this," she said fervently and leaned forward in the chair. "I could never kill anyone. I definitely couldn't stab a man to death. I'm innocent, Mr. Monroe. I would have no reason to kill Wesley."

"Please, make it Nick. Why don't we start by you telling me what happened on Saturday night. Start with when you first got to the Voodoo Lounge. Why did you go there?"

"I'd had my store open late and just decided to go have a drink or two before heading home. Occasionally on Saturday nights, I do that."

At least her tears had stopped. "What happened when you got there?" Nick asked.

She frowned, the gesture doing nothing to detract from her beauty. "It was fairly crowded, but I spied a stool at the bar, and so that's where I sat. From that vantage point, if I turned on the stool, I could see the dance floor, and I always enjoyed watching people dance."

"And who was next to you at the bar?"

"Wesley was on one side of me, and Beau Bardot was on the other side. I ordered a strawberry daiquiri. I visited with Beau for a little while, and then Wesley and I chatted."

"What did you two talk about?" Nick asked as he began writing down notes.

"Nothing in particular…the weather and things going on in town."

"Were you interested in him romantically?"

Her eyes widened. "Heavens no, besides Wesley is… was married."

"Do you have a significant other?" Nick asked. It might be helpful to the defense if she had a steady boyfriend.

"No, there's nobody in my life right now," she replied.

"And you weren't having a secret affair with Wesley?"

She looked at him in horror. "No, I would never have an affair with a married man. Wesley was only a casual acquaintance to me, nothing more. I don't know who killed him. I don't even know how I got into that alley. The last thing I remember is sitting at the bar and sipping on my second drink."

Tears once again shone in her eyes. "I don't know what happened that night. It's all a blank, but I know I didn't do this. I had absolutely no reason to hurt Wesley, and in any case I could never kill anyone."

She swiped the tears from her eyes. "Please, Mr. Monroe… Nick, will you help me? I have some money tucked back, and I'll pledge my future earnings to you. Whatever it takes, I want… I need you to represent me."

"We can talk about payment later," Nick replied. "You're being arraigned this afternoon, and I'll represent you in that process."

"Thank you," she replied in obvious relief. "So, what happens there?"

"The main thing for you to remember is I do most of the talking. You will stand or sit next to me, and you don't need to say a word unless the judge asks you a direct question. Even then, you will consult with me before giving a response."

"Okay, I can do that," she replied tremulously.

Nick got to his feet. "I think we're done here for now. I'll meet you at the courthouse this afternoon right before the arraignment."

She stood as well. "Thank you so much for your help."

"If I do decide to represent you in this case, you have to understand that I'm no miracle worker. You're facing some serious charges, and the evidence against you is very damning. The prosecutor's case is that you were having an affair with Wesley, and when he refused to leave his wife, you killed him."

She looked at him in horror. "All I can tell you is I'm innocent," she replied with a lift of her chin. "There was no affair, and I didn't kill anyone."

"We'll talk more once the arraignment is over."

Nick walked over to the door and knocked to let the officer outside know they were finished. Once she was escorted out of the room, Nick sat back down at the table.

Everyone always proclaimed their innocence when they were arrested, but in this case, Nick leaned toward believing her. First of all, physically, it was difficult for him to believe that a woman of her small stature had managed to stab a man to death. Wesley was a tall, big man, making it even more difficult for Nick to believe in her guilt.

There had just been something about her that made him believe she was innocent. If he was right about her, then the last thing he wanted to see was an innocent woman railroaded for a crime she didn't commit.

That meant somewhere out there in the small town of Crystal Cove, Louisiana, was a cunning killer who had not only gotten away with a cold-blooded murder, but had also managed to thoroughly frame an innocent woman.

Chapter Two

"Ms. LaCrae has no passport and no financial resources to flee. In fact, she's an innocent woman who is eager to stand and fight these charges against her. Therefore, I request that she be released on her own recognizance," Nick said to Judge Henry Cooke.

"Your honor, this is absolutely outrageous," Prosecutor Tommy Radcliffe exclaimed loudly. "This woman is charged with a monstrous murder. Beneath her pretty face is a calculating, cunning person who had an affair with the victim. When he wouldn't leave his wife for her, she took a knife and stabbed him not once, not twice, but three times to murder him." Tommy hit his desk three times for emphasis. "I want her remanded until she stands trial."

Nick felt Heather's outrage as she stood stiffly beside him, but thankfully she didn't say anything to protest what Tommy had said.

She had met with him just minutes before these proceedings. She was still clad in her sweat pants and pink T-shirt. She looked exhausted and stressed. She'd been given her hairbrush and had quickly run it through her long, dark, rich-looking tresses. Then they'd been called into the courtroom.

"Mr. Radcliffe, save your histrionics for the trial," Judge Cooke replied dryly.

"Your Honor, Ms. LaCrae owns a small business here in town and is a solid member of the community. However, posting any kind of bail would be a hardship for her. She is no danger to society."

Judge Cooke pulled on his white beard and frowned. He looked at Tommy and then back at Nick and Heather. "Okay, I hope I don't regret this. I hereby order that Heather LaCrae be released on her own recognizance. Trial date is set for one month from today, and we are done here." He banged down his gavel.

Nick remained standing with Heather by his side as the portly Radcliffe closed his briefcase and then approached them. "You won this round today, slick Nick, but don't expect a success at trial."

"We'll see, Tommy. We'll see," Nick replied easily. He and Tommy had butted heads many times in trial, and Nick wasn't worried about doing it once again.

"So, what happens now?" Heather asked once it was just the two of them left in the courtroom. "Do I have to go back to jail?"

"No, it means you don't have to go back to jail," Nick replied. "You're free to go home right now."

To his stunned surprise, she threw her arms around his neck and gave him a big hug. "Thank you, thank you," she whispered against his neck and then stepped away from him.

"You're welcome," he replied. He had to admit, to

his surprise, her hug felt good. It had been a very long time since Nick had been hugged by anyone. "Do you have a ride home?"

"If I could use your cell phone, I can call my friend Lucy, and she will come to get me when she can. The police kept my phone for evidence. I guess I'll have to see about getting another one."

"You will definitely need one so you and I can keep in touch. In the meantime, I've got nothing going on right now. I can take you home," Nick replied.

"You've already done so much for me. I hate to bother you anymore," she protested.

"Nonsense, it's not a bother. Besides, on the drive, we can talk a little more about the case."

"Does this mean you're going to represent me through the whole case?" Her lovely eyes gazed up at him with obvious hope.

"It does. Now, let's get you home." They left the courtroom and then walked out into the heat and humidity of the day. He led her to his car and opened the passenger door to usher her in. He then walked around the car and got in behind the steering wheel.

"Okay, what directions do I need?" he asked as he pulled away from the curb.

"Do you know where the big parking lot is, next to the swamp's largest entrance?"

"I do," he replied.

"If you can drop me there then I can walk in to my place."

"Got it," he replied. They rode for a few minutes in

silence. He cast her several surreptitious gazes, drawn to her beauty.

Beneath her pretty face is a calculating, cunning person. Tommy's words replayed in his mind. Nick glanced over at her once again. She certainly didn't appear to be that woman right now. She looked small and fragile. He'd noticed earlier that while she had lovely hands, two of her fingernails appeared chewed to the quick. Did calculating killers bite their fingernails?

"Do you have a car?" he asked curiously as he approached the parking area in front of the looming swamp.

"I do," she replied.

"Could you meet me at my office tomorrow morning around ten? We need to get the paperwork taken care of for me to officially represent you, among other things."

"I'll be there," she replied.

"Do you know where my office is?"

She flashed him a quick smile. It was the first real smile he'd seen from her, and it shot an unexpected rivulet of warmth through him. "No, but trust me, I'll find it."

He returned her smile. "My office is at 221 Main Street. I'm right next to Bella's Ice Cream Parlor."

"I definitely know where that is," she replied. "My friend Lucy and I indulge in ice cream way too often." As he parked the car, she took off her seat belt and turned to look at him. "Thank you, Nick."

"Don't thank me yet. We have a big challenge ahead of us."

Her smile instantly vanished. "I'm aware of that. At least I don't have to spend another night in jail. Well, thank you for bringing me home, and I'll see you to-morrow morning."

"Okay, see you then." She got out of the car, and he watched as she walked toward the jungle-like marsh and quickly vanished from his view, swallowed up by the swamp she lived in.

He turned his car around, his thoughts still on the woman he'd just left. The women he'd encountered who lived in the swamp fascinated him. The few he had defended on misdemeanor charges had been incredibly strong women who had to work hard to survive.

He'd never been to any of the shanties where they lived, but he imagined they were quite primitive. No matter how she lived, he hoped Heather had a strong support system in the swamp. Etienne had told him that her parents had passed, and she had no siblings.

Still, from what he had heard, the people who lived in the swamp had become a closer-knit community in the past few months. They all had a common enemy to fear. Someplace in the swamp, there was a man the newspaper had dubbed the Swamp Soul Stealer. So far, he had kidnapped two men and three women, and nobody knew whether the people he had taken were dead or still alive.

There was more hope they were alive since one of the women had turned up. Colette Broussard had been found half dead at the edge of the swamp. She'd been badly beaten and apparently had been starved. She had also been dangerously dehydrated and now remained in a medically induced coma. She had been gone for three months when she'd been found.

The hope was that when she was a little better, she would be able to tell Etienne who had taken her, where she had been held and the condition of the other captives.

However, he couldn't think about that right now. He had to find a defense for a woman charged with murder and facing years in prison and possibly the death penalty. He had to find a way to defend a woman who didn't know how she got soaked in the victim's blood, holding the murder weapon in her hand, with a confession typed into her phone.

He thought about that confession now. It had been fairly simple. *I killed Wesley. I loved him but he refused to leave his wife, so I stabbed him to death and I can't live with myself.* If not her, then who had left that damning message in her phone?

All he knew for sure was that her defense that she was innocent and she didn't remember anything that had happened certainly wasn't enough to keep her out of prison.

HEATHER RACED TOWARD the tangled growth she called home. The swamp seemed to embrace her as she ran down first one trail and then another to get to her shanty.

She wanted to hug the cypress trees she passed with their knobby knees poking out of the dark pools of water. She drew in deep lungfuls of the air that smelled of myriad plants and mysterious flowers and the everpresent faint scent of decay.

She needed to embrace all that was the swamp in

case there came a time when she couldn't be here. Her heart squeezed tight at the very thought of spending years in a prison and away from this place that fed her soul.

Her shanty came into view, and she raced across the bridge that would take her to her front door. Once inside, she collapsed on the sofa. She was exhausted, first from the sleepless night in the jail cell and then from the stress of her time before the judge.

Despite her exhaustion, she was too wired to rest. She sat for only a moment and then got up and went into her kitchen, part of which had been transformed into an herb garden.

In here, the scents of basil and parsley, of mint and thyme, were redolent in the air, along with half a dozen other fragrant herbs.

She went out the back door and started her generator, then went inside and turned on the lights that helped the growing plants flourish. She could only run the lights for about two hours a day, but it, along with the natural sunlight that shone through the windows, was enough to keep them healthy and thriving.

When the fledgling plants got big enough, she would take them into her little store off Main Street. It took her fifteen minutes or so to water them all, and she had just finished when a knock fell on her door.

She opened the door to her best friend, Lucy Dupree. The short-haired, slightly plump woman immediately wrapped her arms around Heather and held her tight. "Are you okay?" She finally released Heather, but grabbed her hand and pulled her down on the sofa next to her. Her brown eyes gazed at Heather worriedly.

"I'm fine for now," Heather replied.

"What the hell, Heather?" Lucy squeezed her hand and then released it. "It's going all around town that you stabbed Wesley Simone in a fit of passion and then took drugs to commit suicide. How on earth did this happen? I know you didn't… I mean I know you couldn't stab anyone. And I definitely know you weren't romantically involved with Wesley Simone unless you've been keeping some major secrets from me."

"Trust me, I certainly have no secrets like that. I would never get involved with a married man, and in any case, Wesley definitely wasn't my type. I don't know how this all happened. I have no memory of that night. My first conscious moment was waking up handcuffed to a hospital bed. I was drugged, Lucy. Somebody drugged me and set me up to take the fall for Wesley's murder."

"Who would do that?" Lucy frowned.

"I wish I knew."

"At least you're home today," Lucy replied. "And that means you must have a good lawyer."

"Nick Monroe, and time will tell just how good he is. So far, I'm impressed with him," Heather replied. "Do you know him?"

"I don't think so, although I might have waited on him at the café at one time or another. What does he look like?"

"Very nice looking…with dark hair and blue eyes." Among the many things that had happened to her, Nick had been yet another surprise. She wasn't sure what she'd expected of the defense attorney, but the very hot man with dark hair and piercing blue eyes had not been what she'd anticipated.

Nick Monroe was definitely a hunk. His attractive facial features were boldly sculpted, and when he smiled, twin dimples had danced in his cheeks.

He'd worn a black suit to court, and she could tell his shoulders were broad and his hips were slim. But it didn't matter how hot he was. What she needed from him was his legal mind. She was depending on him to get her out of this horrid mess she found herself in.

"Hmm, I don't know, that could describe lots of men who come into the café," Lucy replied. "As long as he can get you out of these charges against you, that's all that really matters."

"I agree," Heather replied. For the next hour, the two talked about the charges against Heather. "We really haven't talked much yet about my defense, but the only way I see that I can get off is if we find the real killer," Heather said. "Somehow I need to remember things that happened that night in the bar."

"And how do you intend to find the real killer?" Lucy asked.

"I don't know. All I do know is I don't want to spend a minute in prison for a crime I didn't commit," Heather replied fervently. "One night in that awful jail was more than enough for me."

It was soon after that when Lucy left. For dinner, Heather fried up some fish, and then she turned off the generator. By eight o'clock, her exhaustion finally overwhelmed her, and she got into bed.

The croak of bullfrogs sounded, along with the gentle lapping of water against the stilts that held her shanty up out of the swamp waters. It was the soothing rhythms of home, but on this night, it pulled tears to her eyes. Would she really go to prison for a crime she didn't commit? After her trial, would she never again hear the sounds of the sweet lullabies of home?

Chapter Three

Heather found a parking space on Main just down the street from Nick's office. She shut off her car but remained seated. She was a little early for her appointment with him, but at least she'd already accomplished getting a new cell phone. What she hadn't accomplished was remembering anything that might help her case.

She sat for several long moments, and then realizing it was almost time to go in, she smoothed down the peasant-style white blouse she wore. She'd paired it with a red-and-white long flowy skirt and a pair of white sandals. She'd dressed with the intention of opening her store after this meeting.

Anxiety filled her as she thought about going to the store to work. By now most people in town would know that she'd been arrested and charged with Wesley's murder. They might believe she'd been having an affair with him and had killed him. She had no idea how people would react to her now.

She gazed up the block. Crystal Cove was a charming little town with the buildings along Main Street painted in pinks, yellows and turquoises. People walked along the sidewalk, laughing and seemingly without a worry in the world. Her heart clenched. That was the way she had been before she was charged with murder.

She got out of the car and walked toward Nick's office, her stomach muscles tight with anxiety. Monroe Law was on the front window in neat, silver letters. She opened the door and went inside, where a woman with short, curly reddish-brown hair and brown eyes sat behind a desk.

"Hello, I'm Heather LaCrae and I'm here to see Mr. Monroe," Heather said.

"Hi, Heather, I'm Sharon Benoit, the coffee-fetching, brainstorming, paralegal receptionist." She smiled at Heather. "Now I'll just go back and see if they're ready for you." She got up and disappeared through a doorway just to the right of her desk.

They? Did Nick have a partner? Partners? As far as Heather was concerned, the more the merrier when it came to her defense. She waited only a minute or two, and then Sharon returned. "Just go through the door, and they're in Nick's office...the first doorway on the left."

"Thank you," Heather replied. A new wave of anxiety swept over her as she pushed through the door that led into the interior of the building. She knew she had no real defense. She could only hope that her lawyer came up with something to keep her out of prison.

She came to the first door on the left and knocked. Nick opened the door and smiled at her. "Ah, good, you're right on time. I like a client who is punctual."

He opened the door wider to allow her entry. He looked totally hot clad in a pair of black slacks and with the sleeves of his white dress shirt rolled up to his elbows. As she walked past him, she smelled the attractive, slightly spicy cologne that she'd noticed the day before.

A big, buff bald man stood from the chair he had been sitting in when she came into the room. He was clad in a pair of jeans and a black T-shirt that stretched taut across his massive chest and shoulders. He also wore a shoulder holster and a gun.

"Heather, this is Bruno Foret, private investigator extraordinaire and my right-hand man when I need him," Nick said.

"Hello, Mr. Foret," she replied to the big, intimidating man.

"Call me Bruno," he said in a deep, gravelly voice.

She nodded, then Nick gestured her toward a chair in front of his desk. She eased down into the chair, and then the two men sat.

"How are you feeling this morning?" Nick asked her.

"Nervous…anxious and worried," she replied honestly.

Nick nodded, as if unsurprised by her answer. "First of all, I have some paperwork for you to sign." He reached for several papers on the left of his desk and then stood to hand them and a pen to her. "Take your time reading through them, and if you have any questions, feel free to ask."

For the next few minutes, she read through the documents, the first granting Nick the right to represent her in all matters pertaining to the current charges against her, which she signed and handed back to him. She assumed it was for the court.

The second document was a contract between her and Nick. It also granted him the right to represent her. It stated that he was working the case pro bono. When she read this, she looked back up at him.

"I don't expect you to do this for free, Nick. I told you I have a little bit of money put away, and I can pledge you more from my future store earnings." She raised her chin slightly. "I don't want to be a charity case."

"You sell all kinds of herbs in your store, right?" he asked.

"Right," she replied.

"I like to cook, so why don't we agree that you will give me herbs in exchange for my services."

"Okay…deal, but you need to write that in here so it's legal." She handed him back the contract unsigned.

"I'll give it to Sharon and have her redo it, and you can sign it tomorrow," Nick replied. "Let's talk about what's going to happen now."

"Okay," she replied. She twisted her hands in her lap, anxious to hear how they were going to fight the murder charge. "But before we do that, I got a new phone this morning, and I should give you my number."

"Definitely." He picked up the cell phone on his desk, and it only took them a few moments to exchange numbers.

"Now," he continued. "The first thing we intend to do is conduct our own investigation of the crime. I believe there was a definite rush to justice in this case, and I intend to argue that in court, but in the meantime, Bruno will go to the Voodoo Lounge to question the bartenders and anyone else who might have been there that night. What I need from you is a list of all the people you remember being there, as we intend to talk to each and every one of them. Somebody had to have seen something that night that might help your defense. Can you take a few minutes to do that before you leave today?"

"Of course, I can do that," she replied.

Nick's blue eyes peered into hers intently. "I expect you to be an active participant in your own defense."

"I'll do whatever I can to help," she replied.

He grinned at her, his dimples flashing in a smile that warmed her from head to toe. "Good," he said.

Great, just what she needed…a mad crush on her lawyer. Surely a handsome, successful man like him had a wife or a significant other. She shoved the inappropriate thoughts away. She was facing a murder charge and thinking about romance. What on earth was wrong with her? Maybe she really had lost her mind.

"Do you have any enemies that you know of?" he asked, the question definitely pulling her back to the current topic.

"No, none," she replied firmly. "I get along with everyone, which is why I don't know why somebody would do this to me."

"You haven't had any disputes with anyone recently, no matter how big or small? Maybe a disgruntled customer at the store?"

She shook her head. "Really, I haven't had any problems with anyone."

Nick stood. "Okay, now I'll just take you to one of the conference rooms so you can write out that list for me." He grabbed a legal pad and pen and gestured for her to follow him.

"It was nice to meet you, Bruno," she said to the big man who had remained silent through the short meeting.

"Oh, I imagine you'll be seeing a lot of me from now on," he replied.

Heather followed Nick down a long hallway and into a small room with a table and four chairs. He handed her the notebook and pen. "Make yourself comfortable. Can I get you a cup of coffee or something else to drink?"

"No, thank you. I'm fine," she replied.

"Then I'll just leave you to get to it. When you're finished, just let Sharon know. I have an appointment with another client in fifteen minutes. It should be a relatively short meeting, and I'll see you after."

With that, he left the room and closed the door behind him. She stared down at the blank page in front of her, for a moment overwhelmed by the task before her.

God, she wished her parents were still alive. Her father had died eighteen months ago from lung cancer, and then six months ago her mother had suffered a massive heart attack and had passed away. Despite being twenty-nine years old, Heather had lived with them.

About the time she'd seriously considered finding her own place, her father had gotten ill. She had remained at home first to help nurse her father and then to support her grieving mother. Now, more than ever, she wished they were here to support and guide her.

She released a deep sigh and turned her thoughts to that night in the Voodoo Lounge. The first names she wrote down were the easy ones. She remembered the people who had been on the dance floor. They were regulars who were there on most Saturday nights. It became more difficult for her after that.

She searched her memory until the time when she had no memory left. Somebody had obviously drugged her drink in an effort to kill Wesley and frame her. Who had been close enough to her at the bar to do that?

There was one thing she did remember. She had done what no smart, single woman should ever do—she'd left her drink unattended when Jason Tremont had asked her to dance. That had to have been when the drink was tampered with. So, who had been around the bar when she had returned to her seat after her time on the dance floor? She needed to tell Nick this piece of information.

She wrote down all the names of the people she could remember and then sat for a few more minutes to see if any more came to her. One thing she did know was the bar had been packed that night, and there had been people there she didn't know by name.

When she finished, she had the names of about fifteen people written down. At least it would be a good place for Bruno to start, and hopefully she'd remember more people as time went on. Somebody had to have seen something that night that would help her.

She left the conference room and went back into the lobby, where Sharon smiled at her. "The meeting Nick is in is running longer than he expected. He said to tell you that he'll meet with you again tomorrow morning at nine."

"Okay, and here's the list he wanted from me." Heather

handed over the legal pad and pen. "And I guess I'll just see you in the morning."

Heather left the office and returned to her car. Once inside, she released a deep sigh. Hopefully Nick and Bruno would be able to find somebody who could corroborate her story. She didn't even want to think about the consequences for her if they were unsuccessful.

"So, WHAT DO you think of Ms. Heather LaCrae?" Nick asked Bruno. Nick had ended his meeting with Tony Bridges, who had been charged with trespassing and criminal mischief. By that time, Heather had left but Bruno hadn't, so he then had called Bruno back into his office. He and the big, muscled man had been good friends since they'd been kids, and Nick valued Bruno's opinion.

"I'm not sure what to think at this point. Could she be totally innocent? Sure. But could she be guilty as hell? Absolutely. She could definitely come off to a jury as a femme fatale. She's drop-dead gorgeous and could have easily seduced Wesley, who is…was a very wealthy man and was married to the crankiest woman in town. Heather could have gotten Wesley drunk enough to follow her into the alley, where she demanded he leave his wife for her, and when he ultimately refused, she stabbed him to death."

"I don't know—I believe she was set up and is totally innocent in all this," Nick replied.

Bruno raised one of his thick, dark eyebrows. "It's awfully early in the game for you to have that opinion." He cast Nick a sly smile. "It doesn't have anything to do with the fact that her big brown eyes gazed at you with unbridled hero worship, does it?"

Nick laughed. "I didn't even notice that."

Bruno shot him a look of disbelief and then stood. "On that note, I'll get out of here and see what I can dig up at the Voodoo Lounge."

"Thanks, Bruno. I'll just talk to you later," Nick replied. The minute Bruno left his office, Nick reared back in his chair thoughtfully.

Was he jumping too quickly to conclusions because he wanted Heather to be innocent? Because she looked small and helpless and had, indeed, looked at him as if he was her hero?

He'd made that mistake before. Her name was Delia Hunter, and she'd been charged with aggravated assault on another woman. According to the prosecution, Delia had broken into Laura Dillon's home in the middle of the night and had beaten her so badly that Laura had suffered numerous serious injuries. The beef between the two women apparently had started when Laura dinged Delia's car in a parking lot.

Delia had been a slender, attractive blond who had insisted she hadn't done the crime. She'd been passionate about her innocence, and immediately Nick had believed her.

As he worked on her case, the two developed an intimate relationship, and Nick had believed himself in love with her. He'd also believed that she was deeply in love with him.

He was ecstatic when he won her defense case, but once that happened, she dropped him like a hot potato and left town with another man. Two years later, he'd heard she'd been arrested for the same kind of crime, and he realized she had probably been guilty when he'd defended her.

Delia had been three years ago, and he certainly didn't intend to make that same kind of mistake with Heather. Bruno was right, it was far too early in the game for him to make sweeping judgments about Heather's innocence.

However, as her defense attorney, it really wasn't his place to determine whether she was guilty or innocent. His job was to defend her to the best of his ability. And in order to do that, he wanted to know more about her. He wanted to know her life inside and out.

With this thought in mind, he got up from his desk, strapped on his gun, pulled on his suit jacket and then grabbed his car keys. Heather's best friend, Lucy, worked as a waitress at the café, and he was in the mood for an early lunch and a little conversation with her. Hopefully, she was working that day.

Even though it was a bit early for the lunch crowd, the Crystal Cove Café was busy. He found a parking space in the lot behind the building and then headed around to the front door.

As he stepped inside the establishment, he was greeted by a number of delicious scents. The smell of frying hamburgers and onions wafted in the air, along with the aroma of seafood and cooking vegetables. There was also the fragrance of freshly baked bread and pastries.

Hopefully Lucy was working, but since he had no

idea what she looked like, he grabbed a table for two and sat. He was in luck, the slightly plump waitress who came to his table had short dark hair, a friendly smile and a name tag that read Lucy.

"Ah, just the woman I wanted to see," he said.

"Are you hungry?" she asked as she placed a glass of water and a menu on the table.

"Yes, both for food and some information. I'm Nick Monroe, and I am the lawyer representing Heather," he explained.

"Oh, Mr. Monroe, it's so nice to meet you. Heather told me all about you. She's totally innocent, you know. I've known her since we were kids, and she isn't capable of hurting anyone. It's simply not in her. She's a wonderfully kind and gentle woman," she said in a quick explosion of words.

"Before I order, I was wondering if there was some place we could go where I could have a short chat with you. Would you be able to take a ten-minute break?"

She frowned and looked around. "We're pretty busy right now. I could take a break after the lunch rush, but I really can't right now. But I want to do whatever I can to help Heather."

Nick nodded, realizing it had been stupid of him to come in for an interview around lunchtime and expect a waitress to stop working. "Why don't I come back around one thirty, and hopefully then you can take a break and talk to me."

"That sounds perfect," she replied. "Now would you like to order something anyway while you're here?"

He ordered a burger and fries, and as he ate, he listened to the gossip that swirled around the room along with the clink of silverware and laughter.

There was no question that the majority of the conversations he could overhear were about the murder and Heather's involvement. The general consensus was that she had to be guilty.

"I guess this just goes to show that you never know what's really going on in somebody's life," a woman at the next table said.

"Poor Millie, she must be reeling. Not only is her husband dead, but she also found out that he was apparently cheating on her with a much younger woman," another woman at the same table replied.

"It doesn't really surprise me at all. After all, she's one of those swamp people who have no morals at all." This was said by Brett Mayfield, a large man who worked as a handyman and building contractor and came from a wealthy family.

It was disheartening that, before the trial even began, apparently most of the people in town had already judged Heather guilty. And it was particularly disheartening that there were still people who were blatantly prejudiced against anyone who came from the swamp. He finished his burger and then lingered over a cup of coffee.

He finally left the café and headed to the police station. He wanted to have another quick chat with Etienne. When he arrived, the chief of police was in his office, and he welcomed Nick in.

"I'm assuming you're here about the murder case," Etienne said.

"I just thought I'd give you a heads-up that as part

of the defense I intend to argue that there was a rush to judgment," Nick said.

Etienne released a small, dry laugh. "Good luck with that. She was caught covered in blood and with the murder weapon in her hand, and let's not forget the confession in her phone."

"She didn't do it, Etienne. Somebody drugged her and then framed her for the murder. Somebody wanted Wesley dead, but it wasn't Heather. I know you have a lot on your plate with the Swamp Soul Stealer, but I would suggest you investigate what was going on in Wesley's life. Bruno and I will be investigating all aspects of this crime."

Etienne released a deep sigh. "It would have been poor police work not to arrest and charge Heather for the crime given all the physical evidence at the scene. It's highly unusual to do an investigation after somebody has already been charged, but I'll tell you what I'll do. I'll try to get a couple of men to look into Wesley's life and see if there's any motive there for somebody else to kill him."

"And if you find out anything, you'll share that information with me?"

"Of course."

"Anything new with Colette?" Nick asked.

Etienne frowned. "She's still in a coma. We're just waiting for her to come out of it. Medically, there's no reason for the coma. The doctors suspect it's trauma that's keeping her from waking up."

"I know you hope she can give you some answers in the Soul Stealer case."

The lawman nodded. "Definitely."

Nick stood. "I'll just get out of here and let you get back to work."

"Thanks, Nick. I'll talk to you later."

Nick left the police station and returned to the café, where he had his chat with Lucy. She told him Heather didn't have a boyfriend, that for much of her adult life she'd been caring first for her sick father and then for her mother.

She painted a picture of a kind and thoughtful woman who had never had problems with anyone. Lucy obviously adored her friend and would make a good character witness for her. Of course, the prosecutor would try to make a case that Lucy would lie for her best friend.

It was just after two when he decided to check out Heather's store. The little shop was housed in a pink building with a sign out front proclaiming the business as Heather's Herbs and Plants.

A bell tinkled to announce his entrance. It was like walking into an enchanted garden with plants hanging overhead and rows of spices and other plants displayed on shelves. Myriad pleasant scents filled the air and Heather greeted him from behind a counter with an old-fashioned register on top of it.

"Nick…what a surprise," she said as she stepped out into the aisle and walked toward him. She smiled, the beautiful gesture surprisingly once again warming him from head to toe.

"I figured I'd stop by and see your shop for myself. Nice place. How's business?"

Her smile instantly fell. "Today, not so good. Nobody has been in, although several people have walked by, stopped and stared inside the front window. I guess I should get used to people staring at me now."

"I'm sorry that's happening to you," he replied sympathetically. She stood close enough to him that he could now smell her scent. It was one of wildflowers with a hint of vanilla, and it was very attractive.

"I'm just hoping that as time goes by, I'll be less of a sensational figure for people to stare at."

Talking about sensational figures, she definitely had one. Her breasts were full and her waist was small. Her hips were slender, but the whole package was definitely sensational.

He frowned inwardly. These were the last kind of thoughts he needed to be having about his client. "Why don't you show me around the place," he said.

For the next twenty minutes or so, he walked with her up and down the two aisles, and as she explained the plants to him it was obvious she loved what she did. Her entire face lit up and her eyes sparkled brightly as she told him about the various herbs. She also looked good in the white blouse and the skirt that swirled around her long legs. He'd noticed that when she had first walked into his office that morning.

"What made you go into this business?" he asked curiously.

"My mother always had a little herb garden, and I saw how people would come to her to get the fresh herbs they wanted to cook with. So, I just decided to expand on what she was doing. I figured there might be a lot of people here in town wanting herbs and plants, and so here I am."

"It's all quite impressive," he replied.

"Why don't I send you home with some of the herbs. All they really need to stay healthy is some sunshine and water." As she spoke, she grabbed a box and began to place some of the plants inside it. "You mentioned you like to cook. It will be nice for you to be able to have on hand some fresh parsley and oregano."

"Whoa, that's enough for today," he said when she had four plants in the box.

"Are you sure?"

"I'm positive," he replied. He took the box from her. "I have a perfect windowsill in my kitchen for these."

"Good," she said with another beautiful smile.

"And now I'll just get out of here. I need to check in with Bruno and see what he's found out." He was instantly sorry that his words stole the smile from her face. "In the meantime, I'll see you in my office in the morning."

She walked toward the door with him, and when they reached it, they both stepped outside into the bright sunshine. "Thanks for stopping by," she said.

"I was intrigued to see what you did here," he replied. "And thanks for the herbs."

He'd barely gotten the words out of his mouth when there was a loud pop and a bullet slammed into the building just to the left of where Heather stood.

Chapter Four

Nick quickly shoved Heather behind him. He dropped the tray of plants to the ground and immediately surprised her by pulling a gun from beneath his sport jacket. Deep gasps of fear escaped her as her brain tried to process the fact that somebody had just shot at them…at her.

Nick's body shielded hers and radiated tension as he remained unmoving, his gun at the ready. They remained that way for several long minutes.

"Get inside," he finally said to her. "Get back into your store and call Etienne. I'll stay right here until he arrives. And if you have a back door, make sure it's locked up." The words fired out of him, and he moved away from her just enough so she could open the shop door.

She escaped inside and went over by the register. Her cell phone was on the counter. Her fingers shook as she punched in the emergency number.

"Crystal Creek Police Department. Officer Smith speaking. How can I help you?" the voice said on the other end of the line.

"This is Heather LaCrae. I… I'm at my shop w-with

Nick Monroe and s-somebody just s-shot at us. We need Chief Savoie here right away." Her voice shook uncontrollably as sheer terror fully gripped her.

"We'll be right there," Officer Smith replied.

Heather hung up and rushed to her back door to make sure it was secured. She returned to the store floor and stood staring at Nick's back just outside. Tears welled up in her eyes as shivers of fear raced up and down her back.

Who had shot at her? There was little question in her mind that the bullet had been meant for her. Had it been one of Wesley's relatives looking for revenge? That night in the Voodoo Lounge, he had bragged on his two grown sons.

Or maybe the bullet had been meant for Nick. Somebody wanted him dead because he dared to defend her. She really had no idea what to believe. All she knew for sure was that chills of fear overtook her. The tears that had burned hot in her eyes now fell down her cheeks.

At that moment, Nick came back into the shop. "Whoever it was, he or she is probably gone by now." He strode toward her and obviously saw her tears.

"Hey…hey, don't cry," he said softly, and then he drew her into his arms and held her. "We're safe and everything is going to be all right. I've got you."

His strong arms embraced her, and his scent filled her head. For just that moment, she felt protected and cared for. He held her for several long moments, his heartbeat strong and steady against her frantic one. The sound of a siren blared from outside, and he finally released his hold on her.

She swiped the tears from her cheeks as the siren stopped, letting them know that the police had arrived. Etienne was the first one in, while an officer Heather didn't know stood outside in front of the door.

"You both okay?" he asked, looking first at Nick and then at Heather.

"We're okay," Nick replied. "Thank God I decided to wear my gun today."

"So, talk to me, Nick," Etienne said tersely. "Tell me exactly what happened."

Nick explained about them walking out of the door and the bullet that slammed into the building far too close to them. "Did you see anyone?" Etienne asked.

"No, in fact I can't even tell you what direction it came from. It was so dammed unexpected," Nick said. Frustration was rife in his tone.

"You two stay in here, and we'll see what we can find outside," Etienne instructed. "I'll be back in to talk to you in a little while."

He left the shop, and Heather went into the little break room at the back and grabbed a folding chair for Nick to use while they waited for Etienne's return. She had a stool behind the register to sit on.

At least some of the abject terror that had tightened the back of her throat and brought on her tears had passed. While she was still scared and unsettled by what had happened, she felt better in control of her emotions.

"Thanks," Nick said as he took the folding chair from her. They both sat, and she finally drew her first real breath since the whole ordeal had occurred. "Are you doing okay?" His blue eyes held a wealth of concern as he gazed at her.

"I'm doing better than I was, but I'm not going to lie. I'm still a bit scared. It's not every day that I get shot at." She released a deep sigh. "I just wish I knew who it was."

"Yeah, me, too," he replied.

"I know Wesley has a couple of grown sons. Maybe one of them wants revenge on me for supposedly killing their father," she speculated.

"Hopefully Etienne will find something that will point to the guilty party. He should be able to retrieve the bullet, and sometimes that can hold some answers. And I'm sure he'll interview Wesley's family to find out where they all were when this happened."

"Excuse me if Etienne isn't my favorite person right now. He's responsible for charging me with a murder I didn't commit," she replied indignantly.

"You can't fault him for doing his job, Heather. Besides, he didn't charge you, the prosecutor did," he replied.

"And now I feel like everyone in town hates me and wants me dead," she said miserably.

"Heather, you know that isn't true. Just because some nut fired a gun at us, that doesn't mean that everyone in town wants you dead." His eyes gazed at her softly. Oh, she could easily fall into those beautiful blue depths. "Etienne will figure this out, just give him a chance."

She sighed and nodded. Her world had been turned upside down, and she had no clue who was responsible. She was frightened not just by the bullet that had come far too close to her head, but also by what her future might hold.

"I forgot to tell you something about last Saturday night when I was in the bar," she said, suddenly remembering she needed to tell him about leaving her drink unattended.

"It was a stupid thing to do," she said once she'd finished telling him. "I guess I just never dreamed that anyone would want to drug me for any reason."

"And you still don't remember anyone being at the bar and around your drink when you returned from the dance floor?"

"No. I'm still trying to remember anything I can about that night."

"Anything you do remember might help your case."

They fell silent for several long minutes. She stared out the shop's front window, where she could see several police officers walking around the cars parked along the street. She could only be so lucky that they would find something that identified the shooter.

It was about an hour later when Etienne came back into the shop to speak to them. "We got the bullet out, and it's in perfect shape to check the striations and see if the gun it came from has been used in another crime. We also found several gum wrappers lying on the ground around where we believe the shooter might have parked. Somebody who chewed spearmint gum was in that parking space for some time."

"And it could have been the shooter just waiting for Heather to step outside. At least that's something to go on," Nick said as he stood.

"We're done here," Etienne said and then looked at Heather. "However, we'll be conducting interviews, especially with Wesley's family members." The lawman frowned. "We're going to do our very best to find this person. I don't like vigilantes, and I suspect that's what this might be. In the meantime, Heather, you need to be observant and watch your surroundings."

"Trust me, I will," she replied. A new shiver raced up her back. "I think I'll close up shop for the rest of the day."

"I'll walk you to your car," Etienne offered.

"And I'll follow you back to the swamp," Nick added.

"Thank you both," she replied as the threat of tears once again pressed heavy against her eyelids. Right now, all she wanted was to be home in her shanty, where she felt safe and secure.

Minutes later, she was in her car and headed toward home. It was a comfort to glance in her rearview mirror and see Nick's car following closely behind hers.

Hopefully Etienne would be able to identify and arrest the guilty party quickly, and there was nobody else in town who might want her dead.

She hoped the wheels of justice moved quickly and fairly, and when this was all over, she would be both alive and free.

DAMMIT, THE BULLET had missed her. He drove away from the flower shop and then turned on Main to head home. She was supposed to have died in that alley with Wesley's bloody body next to her. But he obviously hadn't drugged her enough, and now she was a loose end he couldn't afford.

She had been the perfect patsy, and when she'd walked out on the dance floor, leaving her drink behind on the bar, he knew it was fate. He saw the perfect opportunity to make an example out of Wesley and set the woman up for the murder.

But she'd survived, and now he worried about what she might remember from that night. She apparently hadn't remembered him yet because if she had, he would be in jail already facing charges. But that didn't mean she wouldn't still remember some detail that could eventually see him in jail.

He'd been stupid to take a shot at her while the man had been with her, but he'd been parked for over two hours waiting for her. When they had finally stepped outside, he hadn't been able to help himself. He'd fired one shot, hoping it would hit the mark, but unfortunately it hadn't.

There would be another opportunity with her. He would make sure of it. He couldn't allow her to live, and the sooner he took care of her, the better.

NICK FOLLOWED HER to the area where most of the people who lived in the swamp parked their cars. He suspected one of Wesley's sons had fired that shot at her, and he hoped like hell Etienne managed to get the guilty party into jail for attempted murder. The last thing Heather needed was a grief-crazed vigilante after her.

He now pulled up behind her car and shut off his engine. He got out of his vehicle while she exited hers. He approached her and tried not to think about how wonderful she'd felt in his arms for the brief moments when he'd held her.

Even though he'd been trying to comfort her, he'd still noticed the press of her full breasts against his chest and the way she'd fit perfectly in his arms. It had been a very long time since a woman had stirred him the way she had when he'd embraced her.

She now gazed at him with slightly haunted eyes. "Are you okay?" he asked even though he knew she wasn't. How was she supposed to be all right when somebody had just shot at her?

"I will be," she replied and lifted her chin. "I'm just going to have to watch my back from now on."

"Do you own a gun?" he asked. He now stood close enough that he could smell the evocative scent of her.

"I don't, but my father did, and it's still at my house," she said.

"Do you know how to use it?" he asked.

Her big, doe-like eyes narrowed slightly. "I do."

"You might want to start carrying it with you. I can get you off a charge of possessing and firing a gun that doesn't belong to you better than I can resurrect you from the dead."

A corner of her lush lips turned slightly upward. "Are you telling me you don't have godlike powers?"

He laughed. "Afraid not, although if I did have that kind of power, the first thing I would do is drop the charges against you."

"But what about world peace?"

"That would be the second thing on my agenda," he replied with a small laugh.

She cast him a full smile that ignited a flicker of heat deep inside him. "You're a nice man, Mr. Monroe."

"You won't think that when you see me at trial. I can be a real mean son of a bitch when I'm cross-examining witnesses. Don't mistake me for a nice man, Heather."

"Duly noted," she replied. "And on that note, I'll just see you in your office tomorrow morning." She turned and raced onto the trail that took her into the swamp and quickly out of his sight.

He released a deep sigh and then turned and headed back to his car. He couldn't believe he'd just basically told her he was a jerk, but he found himself incredibly attracted to her and had needed to put up a wall so things would go no further.

He'd been burned once before by a client with winsome eyes and a beautiful smile, and he wasn't about to allow it to happen again. He would defend Heather to the best of his ability, and then they would go their own ways.

Damn, he was overthinking all of this. Just because he'd enjoyed holding her in his arms for a minute didn't mean anything at all other than he was a normal, healthy man. His reaction to her had simply surprised him. And besides, she hadn't given him any indication that she might be interested in him on a personal level.

"Hey, boss," Sharon greeted him as he came back into his office. "I have a little gossip to share with you."

"Come on back," he said.

Moments later he was at his desk, and Sharon sat in a chair before him. "What's up?"

"While you've been gone, I've been trying to find

out what I can about Wesley Simone. Word on the street is he wasn't a very popular guy. According to several sources, he was a real pompous ass. He owns a bunch of rental houses, and he was never reluctant to toss out a family for a late rental payment."

"Sounds like he was a real gem," Nick said with a thoughtful frown. "Tomorrow, see if you can find out the names of people he dislocated recently. Each one of them could be the potential killer."

"Will do," Sharon replied.

"Now you'd better get out of here. It's late and although I thank you for staying, I don't want to give you a reason to tell everyone what an ogre of a boss I am."

She laughed and got up from the chair. "Oh, I've already done that."

He grinned at her. "Get out of here, and I'll see you tomorrow."

Hiring Sharon had been one of the best things he'd ever done for himself. Four years ago, when he'd decided he needed a receptionist, he advertised for one. Several women had applied, but Sharon had been a clear winner. She was a paralegal who knew the law. She was very bright and had a good sense of humor, and she'd definitely been a big asset to him since he'd hired her.

With Sharon gone and the place closed up for the night, Nick got on his phone and called Bruno. Bruno told him he'd come by the office in a half an hour or so.

While waiting for his friend, Nick opened up one of his desk drawers and pulled out a half-empty bottle of brandy and a glass. He should just go home and meet

Bruno there, but lately he'd been reluctant to spend the long hours of the evening all alone in his big house.

Before Delia, he had thrown himself into the dating game. He had dated a lot of women but hadn't found that special one who would fill his life with the kind of love he yearned for. Still, he wanted a wife and a family and was determined to find that particular woman. He thought he'd found her with Delia.

After Delia's betrayal, he'd finally given up and had quit dating altogether. He no longer thought about marriage or a family. At the age of thirty-four, he'd pretty much resigned himself to the fact that he'd probably be alone for the rest of his life, and he'd made peace with that.

He now leaned back in his chair and took a sip of the brandy. The liquor slid down his throat in a smooth burst of warmth. He hoped Bruno was bringing him some information that would help in Heather's defense. He also hoped that Etienne had arrested the person who had shot at her today.

Heather. He took another sip of the brandy as thoughts of his client filled his head. There was no question that he was physically attracted to her, but he certainly didn't intend to act on it. It was a fool's game to mix business with pleasure, and he was no fool.

He sat up straighter as he heard the whoosh of the front door opening. He assumed it was Bruno, who had a key to the office.

A moment later, the big man entered the office. "I'll take one of those," he said and gestured to the bottle of brandy.

"Coming right up," Nick replied. He reached into his drawer and withdrew another glass and then half filled it with the brandy.

"Thanks," Bruno said as he took the drink and then sank down in the chair facing Nick. "So, what's new?"

"We had a little incident at Heather's shop today," Nick said, and then he proceeded to tell Bruno about the bullet that had been fired at Heather.

"What did Etienne have to say about it?"

"He thinks it's a good guess that it was one of Wesley's sons," Nick replied. "I intend to follow up with him tomorrow to see what he found out. So, what's new with you?"

"I talked to Greyson Labone, who is one of the bartenders at the Voodoo Lounge. He was working on Saturday night and remembers seeing Heather that night, but she was at the other end of the bar and was being served by Jeffrey Cooke. I tried to catch up with Cooke all afternoon but had no luck. I'll try again tomorrow." He took a sip of his drink.

"Anything else you discovered?" Nick asked.

"I talked to several people who were on the list that Heather gave you, and while some of them saw Heather at the bar, none of them noticed when she left."

Nick frowned. "Damn, all we need is one person who saw Heather leaving the bar and who was with her."

"I have a lot more people to talk to tomorrow, and in the meantime, I do have a tidbit of rumor information that might tickle your hide."

Nick leaned forward. "And what's that?"

"Word out on the street is that not only was Wesley

a real jerk, but he also had recently begun dabbling in drugs."

"Drugs? What are we talking?" Nick asked as a burst of adrenaline sparked through his veins.

"Snow," Bruno replied, using one of the street names for cocaine.

"Wow, I would have never guessed he was a drug user," Nick said.

"Not only a user, but a seller as well," Bruno added.

Nick's brain worked to process this new information. "How sure are you of your sources?"

"At this point, it's just a whisper of gossip, but I think it's something we need to follow up on," Bruno replied.

"Hell, yes, we need to follow up on this. If this information is true, then we need to find out just how deep he was in this and who he might have owed money to. This definitely could be an alternative theory of the crime."

"I'll dig deeper into all this tomorrow. In the meantime, I intend to hang out at the Voodoo Lounge later tonight and see what else I can find out about our client and her movements that night."

"I don't know what I'd do without you, Bruno," Nick said.

The big man laughed. "I love you, too, bro," he replied. "And on that note, I'm going to get out of here, and I'll see you in the morning." He stood and downed the last of the brandy and then handed Nick the empty glass.

"Don't have too much fun tonight without me, and I'll see you tomorrow," Nick replied.

Minutes later Bruno was gone, and Nick put the bottle of brandy back in the drawer and then carried the two glasses into a small breakroom in the back where there was a table, a coffee machine, a microwave and a sink. He quickly washed the glasses and then dried them and carried them back to his desk drawer to be used again.

It was after eight when he finally headed home. As he drove toward his large four-bedroom house, he thought about everything Bruno had told him.

If it was true that Wesley was using and selling cocaine, then they somehow needed to prove it. He could definitely argue to a jury that Wesley's drug involvement might have been what caused somebody in that same dark world to kill him.

But he needed more than just idle gossip about it. Hell, if he believed all the gossip he'd heard about people in Crystal Cove, then the women who served him in the café were all part of a prostitution ring, and the eighty-year-old city clerk was embezzling millions of dollars a year from city funds.

Gossip was cheap in the small town, and what he needed was facts. It sounded like their investigation was going to go to dark places, and he was definitely willing to go there to save Heather.

Chapter Five

Heather raced toward home, eager to get inside the one place in the world where she felt safe and secure. She still couldn't believe that somebody had shot at her, that a bullet had flown precariously close to her head.

She hoped Etienne now had the guilty party behind bars and nothing like that would ever happen to her again. Still, it had been nice when Nick had pulled her into his arms. In fact, it had been far better than just nice. She had liked being in his arms far too much.

She was almost at the bridge to cross to her front door when a man stepped out of the tangled foliage next to her. "Hey, girl," he said, his unexpected presence making her jump.

"Dammit, Jackson Renee Dupris, you scared the hell out of me," she exclaimed.

The old man's face wrinkled up like a prune as he grinned at her, exposing a missing front tooth. "What did you think? That I was the Swamp Soul Stealer come to get you?"

Nobody knew exactly how old Jackson was, although if she were to guess, she'd say the man was in his late seventies or early eighties. He told people he was as old as the cypress trees in the swamp, and his knees were just as knobby. He made a living by fishing and selling the fish to other locals, and everyone in the swamp knew he had an illegal still and also sold a lot of moonshine.

"I've had a rough morning, Jackson," she said wearily.

"From what I hear, you've had a rough couple of days," he replied. "Anyone who thinks you could kill a man sure don't know you very well."

"Thank you, Jackson."

"You know you have plenty of friends here, *mon petit*. All your neighbors adore you. We can't help you in the courtroom, but we'll do whatever is necessary to keep you safe around here."

She smiled at the old man. "Thanks, Jackson, and now I just want to get inside and relax."

"I'll be keeping my eyes on you and my ear to the ground. I'll let you know if I hear anything that might help you out." He spit a string of tobacco out of the side of his mouth. "Prove to everyone that the no-good Tommy Radcliffe isn't as smart as he thinks he is. That man has been on my ass for years, wanting to get me locked up for selling a little hooch."

"Believe me, there's nothing I want more than for my attorney to make mincemeat out of Mr. Radcliffe," she replied fervently.

Jackson slapped his thigh and grinned at her once again. "Now that's what I like to hear. Okay, get inside and relax, and I'll quit jawing at you."

She smiled. "You can jaw at me anytime, Jackson."

Minutes later she was inside her shanty, where she sat back on her sofa and just breathed. It had definitely been a long, eventful day, and she had no idea what to expect going forward. Would somebody shoot at her again? Would somebody try to kill her again tomorrow?

She jumped up from the sofa, refusing to allow these kinds of negative thoughts to fill her head. Tomorrow she would carry her daddy's gun with her, and if necessary, she would use it to defend herself from anyone meaning her harm. In the meantime, she had plants to watch over and dinner to make.

The next morning at ten till nine, she walked into Nick's building, where Sharon greeted her brightly and told her to go on into Nick's office.

Nick and Bruno were in the room; Nick sat behind his large desk, and Bruno was in a chair in front of him. "Good morning," Nick said with a smile as he gestured to the empty chair next to Bruno's. Those flashing dimples stirred a spark deep in the pit of her stomach. He had such an amazing smile. "How are you feeling today?" he asked as she sat.

"So far, so good," she replied and set her oversize purse on the floor next to her. There was no man who wore a pair of tailored slacks better than Nick. Today he also wore a light blue dress shirt that did amazing things to his eyes. "At least nobody has shot at me so far today."

"Well, that's a good start to the day," Nick replied with a smile. "I spoke to Etienne early this morning, and he said he was still investigating the shooting from yesterday. He'd spoken to one of Wesley's sons but hadn't been able to make contact with the other one. He intends to chase him down today and question him, and hopefully he'll have some information for us by noon."

"I certainly hope so," she replied. "In the meantime, I've got something in my purse that I'll use for self-defense."

Bruno released a small, obviously skeptical laugh. "It's only good if you're willing to pull it out and use it."

She glared at him. "Believe me, if I need to protect myself, I'll definitely pull it out and use it." She held the big man's gaze challengingly for a long moment.

"Heather, I have the revised paperwork for you to sign. Read it over, and if you find it acceptable, then sign it and we'll get it out of the way," Nick said.

She got up and took the papers he held out to her. She sat back down and quickly read them over. It was the same as what he'd given her the day before, but under the terms of payment they'd added in that she would provide him with four plants a month for the next two years.

Even though it wouldn't begin to pay him for his services, at least she was now not a pro bono case, and so she was satisfied. She signed it and then handed it back to him.

"Now we can get down to the real business," Nick said. "Have you remembered anything more about that night at the bar?"

She wished she could tell him something…anything, but she couldn't. She shook her head. "I'm sorry, but I haven't remembered anything more."

"Just keep trying," he replied. "Bruno spent yesterday evening at the bar."

"I talked with several people who were there that night. Most of them remember seeing you there, but they didn't notice when you left and with whom," Bruno said. "If you were drugged up, then somebody had to escort or carry you out the back door and into that alley."

She got the distinct feeling that the big man didn't believe her story...that he believed she was guilty. What did Nick really believe? Did he think she was a liar and a murderer?

It was important to her that Nick believed her, not just because he was her defense lawyer, but also because he was a man she admired, and she wanted him to know what kind of a woman she really was.

"Bruno will keep talking to people. Somebody had to have seen you leave that night," Nick said. "It's just a matter of finding the right person."

"I know the bar was crowded that night. Usually when I went there, I only had one drink and I stayed for a couple of hours and then left," she said. "I don't know how long I stayed on that night. But I was there long enough to have two drinks."

"We'll try to piece together things with witnesses who were there that night. Bruno also heard a bit of nasty gossip about Wesley," Nick said.

"What's that?" she asked curiously.

"I heard that he was using and selling cocaine," Bruno said.

"Wesley? I find that really hard to believe," she said

in surprise. "I thought he was a successful business-man. Why on earth would he get involved in some-thing like that?"

"It's just a rumor, but it's one we need to check out. If he was a player in the drug world, then it's possible somebody from that world was the person who killed him," Nick said.

Suddenly a flash of memory shot off in her head. "He fought with somebody at the bar that night," she said. "I remember, now, him standing by the bathrooms and having loud words with another man. They were definitely having a heated argument."

Nick leaned forward. "Do you remember who he was arguing with?"

She closed her eyes and tried to capture more, but the fleeting memory was gone. She finally looked at Nick. "I'm sorry, but I don't know. It was just a flash of memory. Maybe more will eventually come to me."

"That's okay. Just keep trying. We've also learned that Wesley wasn't a popular figure around town. He owned some rental properties and was a tough land-lord who often displaced families. We're going to try to find some of those people and see just how angry they might have been with him."

"So, the plan is that I will continue to interview peo-ple from the bar and follow up on the rumors about the drugs," Bruno said. "I'm also going to see if I can con-nect with the families who were displaced by Wesley." He stood. "I'll get started right now, and I'll check in later today."

"He thinks I'm guilty," Heather said the moment the big man left the room.

"Bruno is a skeptic by nature."

"But...but you believe me, right?" she asked and held his gaze worriedly. "Nick, do you believe me?"

"I believe you, Heather," he replied with a soft smile. "We're going to figure out what happened to you that night, and hopefully we'll see the guilty party behind bars. I've got you, Heather," he added with another smile. "Now have you had breakfast?"

She blinked at the swift change of subject. "Uh... no, I haven't."

"Neither have I. So why don't I take you to breakfast at the café."

"Would your wife have a problem with that?" she asked.

"She might, if I had one." He flashed her the big grin that made his dimples appear. "No wife...no girl-friend...nobody to get upset about me taking my client to breakfast this morning. So will you go with me?"

"Okay." Her heart warmed with a delicious heat. *He's my lawyer and nothing more*, she reminded herself as the two of them left the office together. Her brain got the memo, but there was no question that she was eager to get to know him better.

Chapter Six

Nick had no idea why he'd invited her to breakfast, although it probably had something to do with how pretty she looked. She was clad in a pair of dark brown jeans that hugged her slender legs and shapely hips.

She'd paired them with a chocolate brown, long-sleeved button-up blouse that not only showcased her full breasts, but also her big, brown, long-lashed eyes. Her lengthy hair was clasped at the nape of her neck with a gold barrette, and gold hoop earrings completed her look.

She looked sexy as hell, and there was nothing more he'd like to do than unclasp her hair and run his fingers through the silky-looking strands. All he'd been able to think about this morning was how her full lips would taste.

The invitation to breakfast had fallen out of his mouth as if of its own volition. But as he escorted her to his car, he realized he was eager to learn more about her.

"I almost never eat out," she said once they were both in his car and they were headed toward the café.

"I eat out far too often," he replied with a laugh.

"But I thought you told me you love to cook," she replied.

"Oh, I do, but most nights I just don't bother with it. What's the point of making a really good meal when you're the only one there to enjoy it?"

"I certainly understand that sentiment. I also love to cook, but most evenings I just fry up some fish for myself and call it good. I don't go to a lot of trouble just for me."

He pulled into the parking lot at the back of the café and found a space. "This place is always busy in the mornings."

They got out of the car, and he immediately threw his arm around her shoulders and pulled her close against him as he scrutinized the parking lot for any threat of danger.

She fit so neatly against him, and her wildflower and vanilla scent half dizzied his senses. He smiled down at her. "Now, if anyone takes a potshot at you, the odds are good I'll catch the bullet."

She smiled up at him. "And here I thought you'd pulled me close to you because you couldn't resist my charms."

"There's that, too."

They stepped into the café, and he immediately released his hold on her. "There's an empty booth down there." He pointed toward the back of the restaurant.

Heather headed for the booth, and as she walked down the aisle, he was acutely aware of people on either side of her watching her and whispering about her. She raised her chin and straightened her shoulders. When she reached the booth, she slid into the side facing the back of the big room.

Nick sat opposite her and grinned. "Good girl," he said. "You didn't look like a guilty woman walking in. You kept your head held high."

"And why shouldn't I?" she asked. "I am an innocent woman."

At that moment, Lucy appeared at the side of the booth. "Hey, fancy seeing you two here. Breakfast business meeting?" she asked as she placed a glass of ice water before each of them.

"A little business and a little pleasure," Nick replied and smiled at Heather once again.

"That's nice. Now, what can I get for you two?" Lucy asked.

They both ordered coffee, and he got the breakfast special of two eggs, hash browns, sausage and a side of biscuits and gravy. She ordered one egg, bacon and toast. Lucy served their coffee and then left to put their orders in.

"Tell me more about yourself," Nick said.

"What do you want to know?"

"I know you live in the swamp. Do you like it there?"

"Absolutely. It's in my blood...in my very soul. I love being someplace where it's so green, and I even find most of the animals there quite fascinating. The people there are all my family, and they are the kindest, most real people you ever want to meet."

"I'd like to meet some of your friends," he replied. He told himself it was strictly business, but the truth was he'd like to see her in her own element. The way her features had lit up just talking about it had only emphasized her beauty.

"I could arrange a little get-together if you're really interested in meeting them," she said.

"I would definitely be interested," he replied.

"Then how about the day after tomorrow you meet me at the parking lot at the swamp entrance around six thirty in the evening. I'll lead you in, and I'll get my friends to be there so you can meet them all."

He grinned at her. "Okay, it's a date."

Her cheeks pinkened slightly, and she quickly took a sip of her coffee. "Now, tell me something about you. Are you close to your parents?"

The question surprised him, and he hesitated a moment before answering. "It's complicated," he finally replied truthfully. "I would love to be really close to them, but they have always been distant and very busy with their own lives. They travel a lot, and I was mostly raised by nannies."

Her gaze softened sympathetically. "Oh, I'm so sorry."

"Don't be. I survived. I heard from Etienne that you lost both your parents. I'm so sorry for your loss," he said.

"Thank you," she replied.

At that moment, Lucy reappeared with their breakfast orders. "Is there anything else I can get for you?" she asked once their plates were before them.

"I think we're good," Nick replied. "Thanks, Lucy."

"My pleasure," she replied. "Heather, we'll talk later," she added and then left their booth once again.

"I was very close with my parents," Heather said,

picking up the conversation where they had left off. "I miss them a lot, especially now. I wish they were here to give me advice and support. But thank goodness I have my friends."

"Well, that's good."

"Do you have siblings?" she asked.

"No siblings," he replied. "And I know you don't have any, either. So, what do you like to do in your free time?" he asked.

She laughed. It was a musical, attractive sound. "To be honest, I don't even know how to answer that. I like to read and I love getting ice cream. Lucy and I hang out a lot, but most nights by the time I get home from the shop, I don't do much of anything. I have a lot of quiet nights by myself."

"We need to change that. You can't be all work and no play. Now, we'd better eat before this all gets cold."

As they ate, they small-talked about the hot and humid weather that late August always brought, what was going on in town and favorite kinds of music they enjoyed.

She was incredibly easy to talk to, and he found her more and more attractive as the breakfast continued. He told her his favorite dishes to cook, and she told him she thought her fried fish couldn't be beat.

"Ah, but you haven't tasted my chicken piccata yet," he replied with a challenging grin at her.

"And you haven't tasted my smothered skillet steak," she countered, her eyes glittering with what appeared to be suppressed laughter. "Besides, I'm at a distinct disadvantage here because I can only cook on an electric two-burner. I don't have the luxury of an oven or a microwave at my disposal, but I believe I could still beat you at making a tasty dish cooking without them."

He laughed, delighted by her challenging spirit. "We'll have to plan a cook-off in the near future."

"Just tell me when," she replied with another one of her charming laughs.

They lingered over coffee as if both of them were reluctant for the meal to end. He knew he was reluctant to leave as he was definitely enjoying the conversation.

They talked about favorite ice cream flavors and how much she enjoyed dancing. He told her about having two left feet on the dance floor and how much he liked to play chess.

"Bruno and I often play chess when we aren't working a case," he said.

"I've never learned how to play. Maybe you could teach me, and in return I'll teach you how to tear up the dance floor."

He laughed again. "I have a feeling I could teach you chess much quicker than you could teach me to dance."

"I don't know, you might find me a really good teacher, and before long you'll be dancing with the best of them," she replied.

His phone rang, and he pulled it out of his pocket and checked the identification. It was Etienne. "Excuse me," he said to Heather. "I really should take this call."

He'd almost forgotten that Heather was his client and not just a pretty, quick-witted woman he was having a breakfast date with. But seeing Etienne's name slammed him back to reality.

"What's up?" he answered. He listened to what the lawman had to say and then hung up and gazed at Heather solemnly. "Etienne just told me that both of Wesley's sons have solid alibis for the time of the shooting yesterday."

Her eyes appeared to darken as she held his gaze. "So who shot at me?" Her lower lip trembled.

God, he hated to see her so frightened, and he knew what he was about to tell her would only frighten her more. "I think it's very possible it's the person who killed Wesley. He intended for you to die in that alley, but you didn't. He's probably afraid of what you might remember about that night, that maybe you'll remember him being with you in that alley when Wesley was killed."

"But I don't remember him," she replied dismally.

"He doesn't know that, and so he sees you as a threat." He motioned to Lucy for their check. "It's vital that you keep trying to remember. Even the smallest detail might help us to identify him."

As Lucy arrived with their bill, Heather pulled her purse into her lap. "Heather, this is on me. I invited you to breakfast, so I pay."

She hesitated and then nodded. "Okay, just this one time."

Nick paid and they exited the café. Once again, he placed his arm around her shoulders and hugged her close to him until she was safe in the passenger seat of his car.

"I don't want you working at your shop until this issue is resolved," he said as he headed back to his office. "Do you feel safe in your shanty?"

"I do," she replied. "My shanty is deep enough in that it would be hard to find for anyone."

"Then you need to sit tight there. If I need to speak to you, I'll come to you. I can meet you at the parking lot, and you can lead me in until I learn the way to your place."

"That's a lot of trouble for you," she said, obviously unhappy with the entire situation. "And I have people who come into the shop on a regular basis to get their fresh herbs. Nick, they depend on me for them."

He parked the car in front of his office. He unbuckled his seat belt and then turned to look at her. "Are those people worth your life? Heather, a man who cold-bloodedly stabbed another man and set you up to take the fall is now potentially after you. We can't know from what direction this danger might come. If you're sure you are safe in your shanty, then that's where you need to stay until Etienne gets this man arrested. People can do without their fresh herbs until we know you're safe."

"I'll stay at my shanty because I decide," she said a bit sharply.

Had he come off condescending or too domineering? That was the last thing he'd intended. He couldn't help himself. He reached out and caressed his fingers down the side of her face. "Heather, you're what matters here, not the people who frequent your shop or anyone else."

He pulled his hand back. God, what was wrong with him? Here they were talking about a killer after her, and what he really wanted to do in this moment was pull her into his arms and kiss her until all the danger had passed.

"Okay," she replied in capitulation. "I'll sit tight in my shanty until something changes."

"Good, and now I'll follow you to the parking lot at the swamp," he replied.

"My car is parked up there." She pointed up the street, and he saw her vehicle against the curb about three spaces up. He buckled up and then started his car again and pulled up next to hers.

She unbuckled and then grabbed her keys from her purse.

"Thank you for breakfast," she said as she opened his car door and prepared to leave.

"I enjoyed it. And in the meantime, I'll be in touch with you by phone with any updates in the case. I know it's ridiculous to say, but try not to worry."

She offered him a small smile. "Okay, and while I'm at it, I'll try not to breathe, either. Thank you for breakfast, Nick. I really enjoyed it."

"Me, too. I'll definitely see you the day after tomorrow."

She nodded and then got out of his car and into hers. He followed her out of town, his gaze shooting left and right looking for any sign of impending danger that might come her way.

He'd hoped the person who had shot at her the day before had been one of Wesley's sons, and Etienne would be able to immediately arrest the guilty party. Unfortunately, it hadn't been one of the sons, and it was a good bet it had been Wesley's murderer.

If he'd had any doubt about her innocence before, it

was gone now. His worry now wasn't just keeping her out of prison, it was keeping her alive.

Heather walked through the shanty, checking to make sure everything was ready for an evening with her friends…an evening when Nick would be here.

Nick…even with everything that was going on in her life, she couldn't stop thinking about him and not just as her lawyer, but rather as a very handsome man she was definitely attracted to.

She'd enjoyed the breakfast she'd shared with him so much. She'd found him warm with a wonderful sense of humor. She'd been drawn to him so much, and when he'd caressed the side of her face, sparks of desire had shot off inside her. And she thought maybe he was drawn to her as well. She saw it in his eyes and had felt it in his touch.

She checked the time and then went into her bedroom, where there was a floor-length mirror on the back of her closet door. She was clad in a pair of jeans that fit her body to perfection, and a red, off-the-shoulder blouse that she knew looked good on her. She'd left her long hair loose, and her makeup was light and natural-looking.

The shanty was completely clean, and she had snacks ready to serve her guests, and it was almost six thirty, the time she and Nick had confirmed earlier in the day through a phone call. Everything was prepared, and she was ready for a nice little house party.

It would be nice to see people. The hours of the days all alone in her shanty had been lonely. However, during that time she'd deep-cleaned the shanty, had read two romance books and had spent a lot of time fishing off her back deck.

The time might have been lonely, but it was also peaceful and restful. She had a feeling she'd need plenty of energy going forward.

She left the shanty and headed down the narrow trails that would take her to the parking lot area. She couldn't help the edge of both excitement and nervousness that bubbled in her veins. She always enjoyed getting together with her neighbors and friends, but her excitement and nervous energy tonight was because Nick would be there.

What would he think about her shanty? More importantly, how would he and her friends interact? Only time would tell.

She moved confidently through the trails, having lived in the swamp all her life. It took her about ten minutes to reach the clearing. Nick was already there. He wore a wide smile as he got out of his car.

He looked hotter than she'd ever seen him. He was clad in a pair of jeans that fit him as if specifically made for him. He also wore a royal blue polo shirt that showed off his broad shoulders and matched his gorgeous blue eyes.

"Good evening, Heather," he greeted her, causing a wealth of warmth to suffuse her.

"Hi, yourself," she replied.

"It's good to see you alive and well," he said as he approached where she stood.

"So far, so good," she replied. "Are you ready to enter the jungle I call home?"

"Ready and willing," he said.

"Then just follow me." She turned and reentered the narrow paths that would take them back to her home. "Have you ever been in the swamp before?" she asked as they walked.

"No. I've represented a lot of clients from here, but they've always come to me in my office. This is a whole new experience for me."

"I hope you find it a pleasant one," she replied. He walked close enough to her that she could smell the heady scent of his cologne.

"So far, so good," he replied, making her laugh.

She continued to lead him, showing him where to jump to avoid dark pools of water and to duck under the lacy Spanish moss that hung low from some of the trees.

Finally, her shanty came into view. The four-room wooden structure stood on stilts and had trim painted in a dark green that made it meld into the greenery all around it. The early evening sunlight painted everything with a soft, golden glow, making it look like an enchanted cottage.

Together they went across the bridge to the porch that held a rocking chair. She often sat on the porch in the early evenings and watched as daytime animals went to bed and the nighttime animals came out to play.

In the mornings, she sometimes drank her first cup of coffee sitting in the rocking chair as the swamp all around her awakened for the day. It was so beautiful here in the mornings. She unlocked the front door and then opened it and ushered him inside.

"This is really nice," he said as he looked around. She followed his gaze and tried to see the place through his eyes. A tan sofa sat in place in front of the large window. Throw pillows in deep green, brown and rust decorated the sofa. A matching tan chair faced the sofa and a small pot-bellied stove and a bookshelf full of books completed the living room.

Beneath the furniture was a large, braided rug that she and her mother had made together. It was also in the earth-toned colors she loved. To her, the room felt cozy and inviting, and she was pleased to see both a hint of surprise and approval in his eyes. "If you don't mind, can I see the rest of the place?" he asked.

"Of course." She took him to the kitchen area, where much of the space was dedicated to fledgling plants growing. She then showed him her bedroom, where the queen-size bed was covered with a green-flowered spread and the top of her dresser held a jewelry holder and her lotions and perfume. Next was the small bathroom that held only a stool and a sink.

"And I have a shower on the back deck," she explained.

"Then you have water service here?" he asked in surprise.

"I wish," she replied with a laugh. "Everything runs on complicated systems using filtration, rainwater and bottled water. Please, have a seat," she said as they returned to the living room. "The drink of the night is beer. Can I get you one?"

"That would be great," he replied and sat in one corner of the sofa.

"Anything new in the case?" she asked as she handed him a chilled bottle of beer from her cooler.

"No, but for tonight we aren't going to talk about any of it. Tonight, we only talk about pleasant things, deal?"

"Deal," she readily agreed.

He twisted the beer top to open it. "So, tell me who all I'll be meeting tonight," he asked and then took a drink of the beer.

She sank down in the chair facing him. "You already know Lucy, and she'll be here. Then there's my closest neighbors on the right side of me, Louis and Becca Bergeron, and the neighbor on my left, Travon Guidry." Before she could say anything more, a knock fell on her door and Lucy came inside.

"I come bearing gifts," she said. She had a bag from the grocery store in her hands. "Seven-layer dip and a bag of chips." She handed the bag to Heather. "Good evening, Mr. Monroe," she said.

"Hi, Lucy, and please make it Nick," he replied.

"Have a seat, Lucy, and I'll grab you a beer," Heather said.

"That sounds great," Lucy replied and sat on the opposite side of the sofa from Nick.

Within minutes, her shanty was filled with her friends and neighbors. There was a total of nine people. She introduced each one of them to Nick, and then they sat on the floor and on the folding chairs she used in her kitchen. Most all of them had brought snacks or additional beer, so there was plenty to eat and drink.

"So, are you going to get our girl off these ridiculous charges against her?" Charles Landry asked. Charles was a big man who often brought Heather fish that he'd caught. He also caught gators for a living. "We all know she's innocent."

"Absolutely, I intend to get her off," Nick replied. "But Heather and I agreed earlier that we're not going to talk about any of that this evening. I'm just looking forward to getting to know you all better."

"Personally, my most favorite topic to talk about is me," Mollie LeBlanc quipped, making everyone laugh. "So, let me kick this off. I'm twenty-six years old and work as a clerk in the grocery store, but secretly I'm waiting for a rich man to sweep me off my feet and get me out of the swamp, preferably to Paris or London."

"Ah, don't listen to her," Becca replied. "What she really wants is to find a good swamp man like I did." She cast an adoring look at her husband, Louis.

"Are you married, Nick?" Brianna Ravines asked.

"No, and I don't have a significant other, either," he replied.

"Well, in that case." Mollie batted her eyes at him. "I've always been partial to lawyers."

Once again everyone laughed. The snacks were brought out to the coffee table, and the conversations continued to flow easily. Heather was pleased that her friends appeared to like Nick, who seemed to be enjoying himself. She felt his gaze lingering on her often, and each time a tiny thrill shot off inside her.

As the evening light began to fade, Heather got up and lit the various kerosene and battery-operated lamps around the room, giving it a soft glow as darkness fell outside.

Charles regaled them with his latest gator-catching adventures, and then Nick shared some stories from when he had been young and had worked as a private investigator for a brief time.

"A man hired me to spy on his girlfriend because he thought she was cheating on him. I watched her for several days, and then one night around midnight, I saw her going into her second-story apartment with a man who wasn't her boyfriend. I was well prepared. I had a ladder in my pickup, and I put it up against the side of the building and climbed up so I could see inside her apartment." Nick paused a moment to take a sip of his beer and then continued.

"I was only up there for about ten minutes when the boyfriend arrived on the scene. It was so dark he didn't recognize me. He thought I was your average peeping tom. He dragged me off the ladder and started beating the hell out of me until he finally realized I was the man he had hired to spy on her, but that was the end of my days as a private investigator. I decided it was too dangerous for me."

They all laughed. Heather found this side of Nick so appealing. He was vulnerable and open to everyone. He'd told her he could be a real jerk, but she found that hard to believe. He was so warm and kind to her friends.

It was after that when the conversation turned darker. "I heard through the grapevine this morning that Willie Trahan didn't come home from night fishing last night," Travon said.

"The Swamp Soul Stealer," Lucy whispered the words as if saying the name too loud might conjure up the monster.

"We don't know for sure the monster got him," Mollie protested. "Maybe he just got his nose in some of Jackson's sauce and is somewhere sleeping it off."

"Jackson must be in the same condition because I'm surprised he didn't show up here tonight," Heather said. "He almost always comes around when we all get together."

"I'll check on him before going home tonight. Since he lives alone, nobody would know if he was missing or in trouble," Louis said.

It was about a half an hour later when everyone began to leave. Heather stood at the door to tell her friends good-night and to be safe on the way home. She always worried when they left her house after dark. Nighttime was when the monster came out to kidnap people.

Lucy was the last one to leave, and once she was gone, Heather and Nick were left alone. He got up from the sofa, bent over and began closing up chip bags that were left open on the coffee table.

"Nick, please leave all that," she protested. "I have all night to do cleanup."

He straightened and smiled at her, the smile that dizzied her senses and filled her with an amazing warmth that flowed through her. "Then I suppose I should get out of here, too," he said.

"I'll walk you out."

He frowned and took a step closer to her. "I don't like to think of you walking back here all alone in the dark."

"I can move through the swamp pretty silently, and if I were to be chased, I can either run really fast or find a good hiding place to wait until any danger passes." She smiled. "I'm used to being in the swamp in the daytime and in the night. Besides, I have a murderer trying to kill me, so the Swamp Soul Stealer doesn't bother me at all."

"That's not funny," he replied and took yet another step toward her. His eyes shone with a light she'd never seen before, a light that made her breath catch in the back of her throat and her mouth go dry.

He raised a hand and reached out and stroked it through her hair. "I've been wanting to do that all night long," he murmured softly. "Heather, I'm feeling very unprofessional at the moment."

"And exactly what does that mean?" she asked half breathlessly.

"It means I would really like to kiss you right now," he replied.

"That's nice because I would really like you to kiss me right now," she said.

He gathered her into his arms and took her mouth with his in a kiss that shot a delicious pleasure from her head to her toes. His lips were soft yet held a hunger and demand that was intoxicating.

She opened her mouth to him to allow the kiss to deepen, and his tongue slid in to dance with her own. He pulled her even closer, and she melded herself to him as the kiss intensified and continued.

Heather had never experienced the desire that flooded through her before. She had never felt this level of fire in her veins in the past.

It was him who ended the kiss and took a step back from her. His eyes still shone with what she believed was a hunger for her. He released a deep breath and slowly shook his head. "I'm so sorry, I… I don't know what came over me."

"It's okay," she replied and smiled up at him. "Whatever came over you, came over me as well."

"And now you'd better walk me out of here before it overcomes us again," he replied.

Minutes later, they were on the narrow paths back to the parking area. She had a small flashlight, mostly to light his way through the tangled marsh. A full moon helped as well, shining down a silvery illumination where it pierced through the tree leaves.

They didn't speak but rather moved quietly while the swamp filled with the night sounds of bullfrog croaks and night creatures rustling through the underbrush.

They finally broke through to the clearing. "I really enjoyed meeting your friends, Heather," he said softly when they reached his car. "You are right, they seem like a bunch of warm and real people."

"I think so. And you were a charming addition to the group," she replied.

"Thank you for inviting me into your world." He leaned over and kissed her tenderly on her forehead. "Now you get home safely. In fact, why don't you call me so I know for sure you got home safe and sound."

"Okay, I can do that," she replied. "Good night, Nick."

He opened his car door. "Don't forget to call me."

"I won't."

She watched as he got into his car and pulled away from the parking lot. She couldn't remember the last time anyone had worried about her getting home safely. It felt good…really good.

She turned and headed back home. She moved as quietly as possible, always aware of the potential for danger from the monster who hunted at night.

When she arrived home, she grabbed her phone and made the call to Nick. It was a brief call; she just told him she was safely home, and then they hung up.

Once the call ended, she sank down on the sofa and thought about the night that had just passed. Nick had surprised her on so many levels. She hadn't expected him to be so open and warm to her friends. And she definitely hadn't expected that kiss.

Even thinking about it now shot rivulets of heat through her. She had only dated two men in the years before her father had fallen ill, and none of the kisses she had received from either of them had stirred her so deeply, even though she had given up her virginity to one of them.

Nick was from the upper crust of Crystal Cove. He was an intelligent, incredibly handsome man who could probably have any eligible woman in town, yet he had kissed her with an undeniable passion.

Was he just toying with the swamp woman as a novelty? Several of her girlfriends had shared the experience of being used by some man from town. There was even a legend of a young woman named Marianne who fell in love with a town man. She was only nineteen years old at the time, and she was all alone in the world after her parents had died in a car wreck.

Marianne had poured all her love into the man, and when she discovered herself pregnant, she couldn't wait to tell him. She had been sure he loved her, too. But when she told him the news, he confessed that he was just using her as a sidepiece while he courted a proper, respectable woman in town.

He told her he wanted nothing to do with her or the baby. Marianne had been devastated, and a week later her body was found hanging from a tree in the swamp. Marianne's story was a cautionary tale mothers in the swamp told their daughters.

Heather didn't want to believe Nick was that kind of man. She needed him to keep her out of prison, but she wouldn't mind if he cared a little about her in the process. No, she didn't believe Nick was the type of man to toy with a woman's affection, but ultimately only time would tell.

HE'D WATCHED THEM saying goodbye at the attorney's car in the clearing. He'd been in the parking lot for some time, staring at the swamp's tangled entrance.

The last thing he wanted to do was go into the swamp with its snakes and gators, but he needed to face his fear of the place to find out exactly where she lived.

He hadn't really expected to see her tonight, but when she'd walked out with Nick Monroe, his heartbeat accelerated and his blood began to boil. She needed to die. But he wasn't ready to take her down tonight.

She might get away from him and hide in the swamp, and the last thing he wanted to do was hunt for a woman in the dark in the swamp. Besides, he hadn't brought his mask with him. He would be vulnerable to someone seeing him and being able to identify him.

No, tonight was strictly a recognizance mission. When the attorney finally left, she turned and headed back into the swamp. He got out of his car and quickly followed her, keeping his distance so she wouldn't discover his presence behind her.

He followed her up one trail and then on another one, trying to remember the exact paths she took so he could repeat this trek when he was ready.

He tried not to freak out as rustling sounds came from the underbrush on either side of him and Spanish moss danced on his face like a thousand spider webs. How could anyone live in a place like this? A place where there were wild boars and all kinds of animals that could hurt or kill a person. Unfortunately, he couldn't depend on a gator eating her. He had to take care of her himself.

Finally, he watched her cross a bridge and go into a shanty. She was now home, and he now knew where she lived. As he turned to make his way back to where his car was parked, his heart beat with excitement.

Now that he knew where she lived, he and a couple of his buddies would pay her a little visit very soon. And when they left her shanty, she would be dead and no longer a loose end for him to worry about.

Chapter Seven

Nick and Bruno sat down the street from a run-down house where rumor had it a lot of drug trafficking occurred. It was after midnight, and so far, there had been little happening.

The house was located in a relatively nice neighborhood. The suspected drug house's shoddy condition spoke of neglect and was definitely an eyesore amid the other well-kept homes on the block.

What Nick was trying to do was identify the drug players in town. It was quite possible one of them had murdered Wesley and set up Heather to either die or be arrested. At the very least, one of them could possibly confirm Wesley as a dope dealer. It wasn't Nick's job to solve the crime, but at this point, he believed solving it was the only way to keep Heather out of prison.

"We'll give it another hour or so and then call it a night," he said to the big man in the passenger seat.

"Whatever you decide. I'm just here to protect your ass in case you decide to do something stupid," Bruno replied.

Nick laughed. "I'm not usually a stupid person."

"No, but I've also never seen you so giddy about a client before."

"Giddy? I certainly have not been giddy," he protested with a small laugh.

"I don't know what else you would call it," Bruno replied. "All you talked about yesterday was how much you liked her friends, how cozy and nice you found her shanty. Oh, and let's not forget how hot she looked in a pair of jeans and the red blouse that exposed the tops of her shoulders. Face it, man. You are definitely smitten."

"I… I think I might be," Nick admitted. There was no question that he had been wildly attracted to her the night before last when he'd seen her so relaxed and open among her friends.

The timid, frightened woman he had first met was gone, taken over by a confident, strong woman who was obviously loved and cherished by her friends.

There was definitely no question he was wildly attracted to her. In truth, he couldn't remember ever feeling so physically drawn to a woman. The kiss they had shared had been amazing, and he couldn't help but look forward to a time when he could kiss her again. So yeah, he was definitely smitten and probably a fool as well.

"I just don't want you to get hurt," Bruno said. "You've already been through the wringer once with a client relationship gone bad."

Nick turned to look at his friend in the dim light from a nearby streetlight. "Do you really still believe Heather is guilty? Even with this drug connection taking shape?"

"It doesn't matter at this point whether she's guilty or not. What matters is she's a vulnerable woman who is depending on you. The power balance between you is off. It's possible any feelings she might develop for you will be born out of deep gratitude and nothing more, and once you win her case, she'll be gone from your life."

Nick frowned and once again directed his gaze toward the suspected drug house. After a moment, he returned his gaze to Bruno. "It's not that deep, bro." Just because he desired Heather, it didn't mean he was going to lose his heart to her. He simply refused to do that. It was just physical attraction.

Bruno raised his thick, black brow. "Whatever you say, dude."

NICK THOUGHT ABOUT Bruno's words the next morning as he drove to the police station. He believed the softness she had in her eyes when she gazed at him wasn't mere gratitude. He definitely believed the desire he had tasted on her lips was real and had nothing to do with the client-attorney relationship.

He'd spoken to her half a dozen times since the evening he had spent at her house. Some of their conversations had been light and easy, about things like how she was spending her time at home. They'd also had deeper conversations about the people they had dated in the past, among other subjects.

He was surprised she'd only had two fairly brief relationships before, and he'd shared about some of the women he had gone out with, however he hadn't told her about Delia. For some reason, he'd been reluctant to share anything about the only relationship he'd experienced where his heart had been truly broken.

Shoving all thoughts of romance past and present out of his mind, he parked in front of the police station and exited his car.

He needed to have a serious chat with the chief of police about this whole drug connection. Now that he knew that it was possible Wesley had been into drugs, he intended to lean heavily on Etienne to look into it.

He walked into the lobby, and an officer he didn't know greeted him. The baby-faced young man wore a badge that identified him as J.T. Caldwell.

"I'm here to see Chief Savoie," Nick said.

"And you are?"

"Nick Monroe."

"I'll see if he's available right now." The officer disappeared through a door in the back of his area. A few moments later, he opened the door that led to the inner rooms.

"He's in his office," J.T. said.

"Thanks, I know where it is," Nick replied.

"Come in," Etienne's voice drifted out of the door at Nick's knock.

"You look like hell," Nick said once he was seated before his friend. Lines of stress were evident on Etienne's face, and his eyes appeared dull. The man looked utterly exhausted.

"Well, thanks," Etienne replied. He raked a hand through his thick, dark hair. "I haven't been getting much sleep lately, and to make matters worse another man has disappeared from the swamp."

"Willie Trahan," Nick replied.

Etienne looked at him sharply. "How did you know that? So far, we've managed to keep it out of the news."

Nick explained about sharing an evening with Heather and her friends, and them all talking about the disappearance.

Etienne released a deep sigh. "He's now listed as a missing person, but we all know this damned Swamp Stealer has taken him. So far five people are missing... three men and two women, and we still don't have a clue as to who this creep is or where he might be keeping these people. For all I know, they could all be dead or are being beaten and starved like Colette was."

"And I'm assuming she is still in the coma?"

"Yeah. God, I'm hoping she'll have some answers for us when she wakes up. Now, what can I do for you today?"

"How big is the drug problem here in Crystal Cove?"

Etienne gazed at him in surprise. "There's no question that we have a bit of a drug problem, but I wouldn't say it's huge. Why?"

"Word on the street is Wesley was not only using drugs but he was selling them as well. I now believe it was one of his drug connections who murdered him and set up Heather. I want you to reconsider the murder investigation, Etienne."

A deep frown cut across Etienne's forehead. "Nick, all you have right now is gossip and innuendo. I can't redo a murder case on that basis. Besides, right now I need all my manpower to find a missing man. Word on the street isn't good enough for this. Come back to me with some cold, hard facts about this drug thing and Wesley, and then I'll see about reinvestigating the case."

Disappointment swept through Nick. He'd hoped to get the police back involved with their powers that Nick didn't possess, but apparently that wasn't going to happen right now.

"If I were you, I'd talk to Radcliffe. Tell him your theory of the crime and see if you can convince him to drop the charges against Heather," Etienne suggested.

"Yeah, maybe I'll do that," Nick replied and got up from his chair. "I'll talk to you later," he said and then left the police station.

Talk to Radcliffe. Yeah, right. Nick knew that would be a complete dead end. There was no way the prosecutor would drop the charges when there was so much direct physical evidence pointing at Heather. For him, this case looked like a slam dunk that would add to his résumé if he was successful in winning it.

Somehow, someway, they needed to find somebody who had firsthand knowledge about Wesley's drug abuse and connections. It was the only way he would for sure be able to save Heather.

Thinking of Heather as he headed back to his office, he called her number.

"Good morning, Mr. Monroe," her voice came over the line.

"Good morning to you, Ms. LaCrae," he replied. "And how did you sleep last night?"

"Like a baby," she replied. "And you?"

"Same. I've been thinking about this cooking thing, and I was wondering if maybe this Friday night you'd be up to coming to my place for a little cook-off."

"That sounds like fun, and by then I'm sure I'll be suffering badly from cabin fever and will welcome the change of scenery," she replied.

"Cabin fever that keeps you safe is a good thing," he replied.

"I know," she replied with a sigh.

"Friday night, how about I pick you up around six? I'll provide the food to cook, and we'll see who makes the best dinner. You can text me a grocery list, and I'll make sure you have everything you need."

"Sounds perfect," she said. "I look forward to it."

"Great, then I'll talk to you later," he said, and they ended the call.

He was definitely looking forward to the evening with Heather, but in the meantime, he needed to figure out a way to infiltrate the drug trade going on in Crystal Cove.

EVENING WAS TURNING into night, and Heather was preparing to go to bed. She turned on the battery-operated lamp on her nightstand and then changed from her day clothes to a comfortable lilac-colored nightshirt.

She got into bed and picked up the book she'd been reading over the past couple of days. It was a romance book, and lately it had been far too easy for her to imagine herself as the heroine and Nick as the hero.

She couldn't wait to see him again on Friday night. She'd missed seeing him over the past several days, even though they'd shared many conversations by phone.

Their relationship had deepened through those phone calls where they'd shared their past dating history, his disappointment over never having the kind of love from his parents that he'd needed as a child and her desire to one day have a family.

She had a deep belief in true love. Her parents had given her a beautiful picture in the way they had loved each other through the years until their deaths. She truly believed it had been grief that killed her mother. She had mourned so deeply at Heather's father's passing. Heather knew that her mother had just given up without the man she loved. Heather wanted that same kind of forever love for herself.

She read for a while, but eventually sleep beckoned and she placed the book on the nightstand, and with a deep yawn, she turned out the light.

Shafts of moonlight drifted in through her window, dancing myriad shadows across her ceiling. The distant sound of water lapping and the bullfrogs' songs lulled her. She watched the shadows on the ceiling until her eyelids grew too heavy, and she succumbed to sleep.

She didn't know how long she had been asleep before she suddenly jerked awake. She bolted upright, her heartbeat thundering in her chest and a fight-or-flight adrenaline rushing through her veins. For several long moments, she didn't know what had awakened her. Had it been a horrible nightmare?

She turned on the battery-powered lantern next to the bed and looked around the room. Nothing seemed amiss. Maybe it had been a bad dream that had disrupted her sleep. She certainly had enough issues going on right now to produce a bad dream or two.

A loud boom sounded from her front door and then another boom at her back door. She jumped out of bed with a scream of fear lodged deep in her throat. Somebody was trying to break in!

She didn't need to know exactly who it was to be utterly terrified. It had to be the killer, and from the sound of it, he'd brought his friends.

Another loud bang against her front door dislodged the scream of fear that escaped her. She screamed long and loud as her brain tried to make sense of this. Oh God, she'd thought she was safe here. She'd truly believed he would never find her here in the swamp. But apparently, she had been wrong.

Frustration was added to the mix of emotions roaring inside her as she realized she'd left her purse, with her daddy's gun inside it, on the sofa in the living room. There was no way to retrieve it now. Any second, the front or the back door would come down and the men would be inside.

Once again, terror gripped her chest so tightly it was difficult to draw a breath. It held her inert in place as her brain struggled to find a solution. *Think. Think!* she commanded herself.

She couldn't even call for help because her phone was also in her purse in the living room. Damn, she had to do something. The sound of splintering wood let her know they were almost inside.

She locked the bedroom door and ran to her window

and opened it. Once it was open, she began to scream again. The noise of her shrieks sent birds flying out of the tops of the trees and into the darkened skies.

The sound of more cracking wood filled the night, and then there was a faint shift in the air and she knew the door had been broken open.

Oh God, they were inside the shanty. Tears began to course down her cheeks as the first bang sounded against her bedroom door. There was only a flimsy lock on this door. It would easily be broken. They would be inside with her in the bedroom in a matter of seconds.

Sobbing, she tried to shove her dresser in front of the doorway. Bangs continued at the door, loud booms that echoed in her very soul.

"Hey, bitch, come on out," a deep voice yelled. "Come out and play with us." Ugly laughter followed the voice.

"Yeah, it's play time, and we're ready to play with you," another voice called out.

"Dead woman walking…that's what you are. But we want to have some fun with you before we make sure you aren't walking or talking anymore." Again, laughter followed the voice.

She tried to ignore the jeers and taunts as she pushed and heaved on the dresser. She continued to sob, desperate to get the large piece of furniture in front of the doorway, but it was too heavy for her to move. The only thing she could do now was scream in abject terror.

She sank down on the edge of her bed, watching and waiting for the moment the door would come down and the men would be inside with her.

Raised voices drifted through her door. Wait…was

that Louis's voice? And Travon? Oh God, had her neighbors come to help her? She jumped up off the bed and listened to the men shouting at each other. There was a scuffling sound, and then there was complete silence, except for the frantic beat of her heart.

A soft knock fell on her bedroom door. "Heather, it's safe now. You can come out." It was Becca, and Heather unlocked her door, opened it and then fell into her friend's arms, sobs of relief coursing through her.

Becca led her to the living room, where not only her neighbors Louis, Travon and Charles stood, but even Jackson, wielding a large, sturdy stick.

"I whacked one of them," the old man said. "I whacked him right over his damned head," he added proudly.

"Thank you," Heather said as she swiped the tears from her cheeks. She sank down on the sofa, and Becca sat next to her and put a comforting arm around her shoulders. The front door hung open, off the hinges, and the wood around it was splintered and broken.

"We heard your screams and knew you were in trouble. There were three of them, Heather, and they were all wearing black ski masks over their faces," Louis explained.

"I tried to hang on to one of them so we could get an identification, but he managed to get away from me," Travon said with obvious frustration.

"I just thank you all for getting out of your beds in the middle of the night to help me," Heather said tremulously.

"You would do the same thing for any of us," Becca

replied. "And now what we need to do is call the police and let them know what's happened here."

"My phone is here," Heather said and pulled her purse off the sofa and into her lap. Her fingers trembled as she took her phone out and punched in the emergency number. "We need the police," she told the dispatcher who answered. "Tell Chief Savoie that it's Heather LaCrae. Some men just broke into my shanty. I'll have somebody meet them at the parking lot to show them the way."

"That sounds like a good job for me," Jackson said once she'd hung up. "It's the one time I'll be happy to see the law."

He left the shanty, and for the first time, Heather released a tremulous sigh of relief. She was safe, but what now? "You're definitely going to need a new front door," Louis said.

"The back door is still intact," Travon said. "But your front door is a total loss. Louis and I can board it up for the time being after the police get here."

"Thank you. I don't know what I'd do without you all," Heather replied.

"You know we're all here for each other, Heather," Becca replied. She got up and went into Heather's bedroom. She returned with a robe for Heather to put on over her nightshirt.

"I'm going to try to find some boards for the front door," Louis said. "You guys stay here, and I'll be back in a few." The big man disappeared out the front door and into the darkness beyond.

"Who were those men?" Becca asked.

Heather released another sigh. "I believe at least one of them was the person who killed Wesley and tried to drug me to death."

"And now he's coming after you," Travon said with a frown. "He's afraid of you and what you might remember about him from the night in the bar."

Heather nodded and raised her finger to her mouth. Chewing her nails was a nasty habit and one she'd tried to quit. She'd started it when her father had fallen ill and she'd sat beside his bedside for hours on end. She only did it now when she was stressed, and she was definitely stressed out in this moment.

It took about thirty minutes for Jackson to finally walk back in, not only with three other police officers and the chief of police, but also with Nick.

The minute she saw him, she got to her feet and began to cry again. In four long strides, he was before her and gathered her into his arms. As she cried into the front of his shirt, she heard Travon explain about hearing her cries for help.

Finally, her sobs ebbed, and Nick led her back to the sofa, where he sat next to her and held her hand tightly in his. She was grateful for his support. The mere familiar scent of his cologne calmed her as she told Etienne her version of what had happened.

"I'm so sorry, Heather," Nick said softly when she was finished. "I was so sure you'd be safe here."

"I thought so, too," she replied.

"I'll have my men fingerprint the door frames to see if we can lift anything," Etienne said. "You've all said they were wearing ski masks, but let's hope they were too stupid to wear gloves."

Louis returned and told her he had the wood necessary to board up the door. Meanwhile, she had fallen strangely numb. The sanctity of her home had been breached by a man who wanted her dead. Where could she go from here? Where could she hide? Who was this man who wanted to kill her? And what was going to happen now?

These important questions flittered through her head but could find no real purchase. It was as if her brain was on overload and had now shut down.

"Go pack a bag." Nick's deep voice penetrated through the fog.

She looked up at him in surprise. "What?"

"Go pack a big bag, you're coming home with me." He squeezed her hand and then released it. "Go on now."

She got up from the sofa and went into her bedroom. She pulled a large duffel bag from the bottom of her closet and opened it on the bed.

At the moment, the idea of staying at Nick's place was overwhelmingly appealing. Somehow, she knew instinctively that she would be safe with him.

The first thing she did was change out of her robe and nightgown and into a pair of jeans and a T-shirt. As she began to pull clothes out of her closet and pack them in her bag, she wondered how long Nick intended for her to stay with him.

Would it be just for a night or two? Yet, he'd told her to pack a big bag. Was that three outfits? Ten? She finally settled on a week's worth of clothing. She added in her toiletries and then zipped up the bag and carried it into the living room. Nick immediately got up from the sofa and took the bag from her hand. "Etienne, are we free to go?" he asked.

"Yes, we can finish up here without the two of you. If I need to speak to Heather again, I'll call and let you know," the lawman replied.

"Don't worry about your front door," Louis said. "Travon and I will take care of things here. You go on now and don't worry about any of this."

Once again, a deep gratitude for her friends brought tears to her eyes. "Thank you all," she said.

Nick threw his arm around her shoulder as they left the shanty. Despite the heat of the night, cold chills raced up and down her spine as she thought of what might have happened tonight if not for her friends. There was no doubt in her mind that if her friends hadn't intervened, she would be dead.

They didn't speak as they hurried down the paths to leave the swamp. Thankfully they encountered nobody and made it safely to Nick's car.

"You're safe now, Heather," he said once they were on their way to his house.

"Thank you," she replied. But for how long was she safe? She certainly wouldn't stay with any of her friends and bring this kind of danger to their doorsteps. It wouldn't take this person long to find her at the little local motel, so she didn't consider that an option, either.

Nick flashed her a long look. "Don't worry about anything, Heather. I've got you."

"I think I'm still in total shock," she replied honestly.

"It had to be terrifying to wake up and hear the sounds of people breaking into your home." His voice was soft with sympathy. "I'm so sorry that happened to you, and I'm so damned mad that I didn't see this coming."

They fell silent once again, and within minutes he pulled up into the driveway of a huge ranch house. It was too dark for her to see the color, but she instinctively knew it was beautiful. The garage door opened and he pulled in.

From the garage, he led her into a large, airy kitchen with attractive gray-and-black granite countertops. "Let's get you settled in for the rest of the night, and we can talk about things in the morning," he said.

From the kitchen, he led her down a long hallway and into the second room on the right. He flipped on the light switch, and a light on a nightstand came on.

The room was beautiful. The queen-size bed was covered in a royal blue bedspread, and the chest of drawers and dresser were rich polished oak. "You should be comfortable in here," he said as he set her bag on the floor next to the bed. "There's an en suite bathroom right there." He pointed to a doorway next to what she assumed was a closet door.

He walked over to where she stood and cupped her face with his hand. She turned her cheek into the warmth of the unexpected caress. "You're safe here. Now get some sleep," he said and then dropped his hand and headed to the bedroom door.

"Let me know if you need anything, otherwise I'll talk to you in the morning. Good night, Heather."

"Good night, Nick," she replied. He left the room and closed the door behind him.

Heather sank down on the edge of the bed, feeling as if she just needed a moment to breathe. She finally stood and opened her bag. She pulled out a fresh night-gown and then went into the adjoining bathroom.

It was also decorated in shades of blue, and she eyed the big tub longingly. If she got a chance before she had to leave here, she would love to take a bath.

However, that was the last thing she wanted to think about tonight. Right now, she just wanted to get into bed and forget that a man who wanted her dead had nearly succeeded tonight.

Chapter Eight

Heather awoke slowly, the night that had passed filling her head. A cold chill swept through her as she remembered the events, but the cold slowly warmed as she also realized she was safe and sound in a bed in Nick's house. She was surprised she hadn't had nightmares all night long, but thankfully her sleep had been dreamless.

She turned over and checked the alarm clock on the nightstand. Last time she had looked at it, it had been a little after three, and now it was a quarter to eight.

Despite the relatively short night, she was ready to get up and face the day. Twenty minutes later, she was clad in a pair of jeans and a light blue T-shirt. She'd washed her face, brushed her teeth and hair, and when she was done, she opened the bedroom door and stepped out into the hallway.

The scent of coffee drifted in the air, letting her know Nick was awake and up. She walked into the large living room and looked around curiously. She hadn't noticed much about it last night when she'd come in.

A large, black overstuffed sofa sat opposite a fireplace, above which a huge television was mounted on the wall. A matching love seat made an L-shaped sitting area. The round coffee table was glass and shiny chrome and held an abstract silver sculpture in the center. There was also a little minibar built into one corner of the room. It was also a lot of chrome and shiny glass. The whole room exuded a quiet wealth and a classiness she found very attractive.

She walked on into the kitchen, where Nick stood at the stove with his back to her as he flipped bacon strips in his skillet. For just a moment, she didn't announce her presence but rather stood and drank in his appearance.

Nobody wore jeans as well as Nick did. They hugged his long legs and cupped his perfect butt. His white T-shirt stretched taut across his shoulders and exposed nicely muscled biceps.

"Good morning," she finally said.

He whirled around and cast her a grin. "Good morning to you. Coffee is in the pot, and I left a cup for you to use there on the counter. I wasn't sure what you'd want for breakfast, but no breakfast is really complete without bacon."

"Please don't go to any trouble on my account, just coffee is fine with me," she replied.

"Nonsense, everyone should start their day with a good breakfast," he said and turned back to the skillet. She walked over to the counter where the coffee maker sat and poured herself a cup of the hot, dark brew. There was a sugar bowl and a little pitcher of cream, and she added a bit of both to her cup.

"Have a seat," he said.

She sat at the large, round glass-topped kitchen table. "Your home is absolutely beautiful," she said.

"Thanks. Most of that is due to an interior decorator who helped me with it all. How did you sleep?" He began to take the bacon out of the pan and placed the crispy strips onto an awaiting plate.

"I slept surprisingly well," she replied. "What about you? Did you sleep okay?"

"I did." He slid the skillet off the burner, poured the excess grease into an awaiting can and then turned to look at her. "Now, one of the most important questions of the day…how do you like your eggs?"

"Any way is fine with me."

"Then how does a mushroom, red pepper and cheese omelet sound?"

"It sounds like a lot of work for you," she said.

He grinned, the dimpled smile causing a spark to shoot off in her heart. "It's no trouble, and I have to confess it's more for me than for you. I love my omelets."

She laughed. "Okay, then. I would love an omelet for breakfast."

"Great."

She watched silently as he went to the refrigerator and grabbed a red pepper and a carton of mushrooms. He washed and then began to dice up the vegetables. He added a couple leaves of sweet basil from the plant she had given him.

"I've never had a man cook for me before," she said once he had the egg concoction in the skillet.

"And I've never had a woman cook for me," he replied.

"Really? None of the women you dated in the past ever offered to fix you a home-cooked meal?" She looked at him in surprise.

"The women I dated were more interested in keeping up with the latest styles and going out to dinner than eating in."

"That's too bad," she replied.

The small chitchat was pleasant, but a bit of anxiety still twisted in her stomach as bigger questions than those about past dating experiences worked around in her head. Questions like how long would she be staying here? When he'd signed on to be her lawyer, he certainly hadn't agreed to her being a guest in his home indefinitely.

Within minutes the omelets were ready, along with the bacon and toast. "This looks delicious," she said as he sat down across from her.

"Dig in while it's hot," he replied. "How are you feeling after last night?" he asked, and then he crunched down on a crispy piece of bacon.

"I'm still in shock that it all happened. I thought for sure I was safe in my shanty. I just wonder how he found me," she replied.

"He had to have followed you in at some point," he replied.

"He's definitely persistent," she said darkly. She fought off a new chill. The idea of this man following her anywhere was horrifying. And what made it even more horrifying was she hadn't even known she was being followed.

"You have him scared," he said.

She released a small laugh. "Trust me, he has me scared, too."

"Well, you don't have to be scared any longer. I have

a good security system, and you'll be safe here until Etienne gets the bad guy behind bars," he replied.

"But, Nick, we don't know when that might happen," she protested. "It could be days...weeks."

He reached across the table and covered her hand with his. "Heather, it doesn't matter how long it takes, you will stay here with me until your life is no longer in jeopardy. Bruno and I can keep you safe. In fact, he should be here in just a few minutes so we can go over logistics. Now, take that frown off your pretty face and finish your omelet. We've got you covered." He pulled his hand back.

"I don't know how I'll ever repay you for your kindness," she said.

He smiled. "You don't get it. Heather, I don't care about repayment for anything. I care about you, and I protect what I care about. Now finish eating before Bruno gets here."

Her heart swelled with relief at the knowledge that he'd allow her to stay here indefinitely. She certainly hadn't expected his kindness and his desire to keep her safe.

They finished the meal, and then she insisted on helping with the cleanup. As they worked to clear the table, their conversation remained light. They talked about favorite foods they liked to cook and various other recipes. He had just put the last dish into the dishwasher when a knock fell on the front door.

"That will be Bruno," Nick said. "Come on, let's move into the living room. Feel free to bring your coffee with you." He picked up his cup, and she picked up hers and followed him out of the kitchen.

She sank down in one corner of the sofa while he walked to the front door. She tensed slightly as Nick came back to the living room followed by the big private investigator. Surely Bruno would believe in her innocence now after what had happened last night.

"Heard you had some trouble last night," he said to her as he sat on the love seat.

"Definitely," she replied, fighting off a new chill as she thought of the night before.

Nick sat on the sofa close to her. "I've told her she'll be safe here until Etienne gets the bastard behind bars. But I'll have to depend on you to help me out with that."

"Whatever you need," Bruno replied without hesitation.

"I don't have a lot going on at the office right now, but I do have a couple of cases that will need some attention," Nick continued. "I don't want Heather left here alone, so I figured when I absolutely have to be in the office in town, you could be here with her."

"I can do that," Bruno replied.

"Is all that really necessary?" Heather asked, hating the fact that from the sounds of it the two men would be babysitting her. "Surely I'll be fine here alone when you need to be at the office," she said to Nick. "You said you had a good security system."

"But it's not infallible," he replied. "Heather, those men found you at your shanty deep in the swamp. They will have no problem finding you here," Nick replied.

His words shot a new chill up her spine. Of course,

he was right. Those men probably already knew she was here. They were probably someplace nearby plotting her demise at this very moment.

"I'm in," Bruno said. "Just tell me when I need to be here, and I will."

Nick smiled at his friend. "I knew I could depend on you. I've got nothing going on for the next couple of days. What work I have to do, I can do from here. But there are a couple of clients who eventually I will need to meet in my office."

"Got it," Bruno said with a nod.

"I didn't even offer you a cup of coffee," Nick said. "Can I get you one?"

"Sure, I could drink a cup," Bruno replied.

Nick got up and left the room, and an awkward silence fell between her and Bruno. She took a sip of her coffee and then lowered the cup and eyed him. "Now do you believe I'm innocent of the charges against me?" she asked.

"Yeah, I think you're innocent," he replied.

She breathed a sigh of relief. For some reason, it was important that he believed her. However, she still felt a hint of disapproval wafting from the big man, and she didn't understand it.

At that moment, Nick came back into the room with a cup of the brew for Bruno. For the next few minutes, the two men talked about the case and the theories of who might be after Heather.

She sat silently and listened to the men talk about what her life had become. Murder and drugs. How had this ever happened to her? That night at the Voodoo

Lounge, all she'd wanted was a relaxing drink after work, but instead she'd been set up by the real killer and now that killer was after her.

A new memory suddenly speared through her brain. "He was rather short but hefty, and he had dark hair," she said with sudden excitement. "I remember now… the man who had heated words with Wesley. But I don't know his name. I'd never seen him before."

"Okay, that's helpful," Nick said. "Would you recognize him if you saw him again?"

"Yes…yes, I believe I would," she replied.

"At least that helps us cut down the suspect list a bit. If that man killed Wesley, then we know it wasn't a tall blond," Bruno replied. "We need to see if we can somehow identify that man. I'll starting asking more questions of the people who were there that night. Surely somebody knows this guy and noticed the two men arguing."

"If they were arguing over drugs, then it's possible we'll see this guy at that house we watched the other night," Nick said.

"What house?" she asked curiously.

"A house where it's rumored a lot of drug trafficking goes on," Bruno said.

"Maybe it's time we watch the house again and bring Heather with us," Nick said to Bruno. "In fact, we should plan to watch that house every night in hopes of seeing that man there."

"Sounds like a plan. If she can point out this guy, then I can work on identifying him," Bruno said.

"So, would you be up to that?" Nick asked her. His blue eyes gazed at her searchingly.

"I'm up for whatever gets the killer behind bars," she replied despite the new chill that danced up her spine. Surveilling a drug house for a killer seemed highly dangerous. What if they were spotted by the bad guys? They could all be killed.

Still, she would agree to almost anything to keep the warm light in Nick's eyes shining on her.

BRUNO LEFT A few minutes later, and Nick returned to his seat in the living room. "I've got to tell you, Heather. I admire how strong you've been through all of this. Most people would have crumbled into a million pieces, but you've stayed steady and strong."

She released a small laugh. "I'm not the type to curl up in a ball and cry, although I've certainly done plenty of crying into the front of your shirts."

He smiled. "And I haven't minded it a bit." He thought about those moments when he'd held her in his arms. Suddenly the memory of the kiss they had shared filled his mind. There was nothing he'd like more than to repeat that experience with her.

"I was thinking maybe tonight I could cook for you. I'll give you the home-cooked meal you've never gotten before," she said.

"I'd be a fool to say no to that," he replied.

"I'll have to see what you have here for me to cook."

"We can go into the kitchen and check it out right now," he replied. "Ready?" He stood.

"Ready," she replied. She also stood with her empty coffee cup in hand.

Together they went back into the kitchen, where she quickly rinsed her cup in the sink and then turned to look at him. He beckoned her to the refrigerator and opened the freezer door.

She looked inside and he stood just behind her. She smelled wonderfully good…of clean woman and the warm perfume he'd come to identify as specifically her own.

"I've got steaks and pork chops. There's a roast and chicken breasts among other things," he said, trying to ignore how her nearness affected him. He had to stop thinking of her as a desirable woman and instead think of her as a client and nothing more.

"I can make you some really good pork chops for tonight," she said and pulled the package of three chops out. He stepped back, and she closed the freezer door and set the package of meat on top of the counter to thaw.

He needed to get a little distance from her before he pulled her into his arms and kissed her until they were both mindless.

"I think I'll take care of a little work in my office. It's in the room across from yours. If you'd like, I can turn on the television in the living room for you."

"Oh, I would definitely like that," she replied. "I never get a chance to watch TV, and some of the women who come into my shop talk about what shows they are watching." It was easy for him to forget that she came from a place where electricity was a rare commodity, and she didn't have many of the things he took for granted.

"Come on into the living room, and I'll set you up with the remote," he said.

Minutes later, he walked down the hallway and then entered the room he used as a home office. The room was painted a soft light gray, and a large black desk held a computer and a fancy printer-fax machine.

He went to the desk and sank down in the comfortable leather chair. He leaned back and thought about everything that was going on with Heather's case.

Were they chasing down the wrong lead with the drug connection? Was it possible that the man Heather saw arguing with Wesley that night wasn't the killer at all? If the murder hadn't been about drugs, then what had it been about?

Beneath all of this was a simmering, inappropriate desire for his client. She'd worn her hair loose today, and from the moment he had greeted her that morning he had wanted to run his hands through the long, silky strands. Throughout breakfast, he'd been on a slow burn for her.

She was so different from all the other women he had dated in the past. She was far more down-to-earth and didn't seem superficial in any way. He would imagine she was a giver, and he'd mostly dated takers in the past.

He shoved thoughts of her out of his head and instead turned on his computer and pulled up his email. Within minutes he was immersed in the business of being a defense lawyer.

He didn't know how long he'd been working when

Heather poked her head in the doorway. "I'm sorry to interrupt you, but I was wondering if you wanted me to make you a sandwich or something for lunch?"

He looked at his wristwatch and was shocked to see that it was almost one. "I didn't realize it had gotten so late. I'll knock off now and come to the kitchen." He saved the document he'd been working on and then got up and followed her to the kitchen.

"I have something to confess to you," she said as he pulled out sliced ham and cheese from the fridge drawer.

"What's that?" he asked. "And sit down, I've got this."

She sat down at the table. "I've not only been watching television, but I also took some time to snoop through your kitchen. In my own defense, I was looking for spices and all the items I need to make you a good meal."

He turned, looked at her and smiled. "I don't have a problem with that at all. In fact, I want you to familiarize yourself with the place you'll be calling home for a while."

He finished making the sandwiches and placed one in front of her and one for himself on the table. "Do you want chips with that?"

"No, this is fine for me." She smiled at him, that beautiful gesture that lifted her lips and sparkled in her lovely eyes. Oh, he could easily fall into the chocolate pools of her dark-lashed eyes.

"I didn't mean to interrupt you so you could fix lunch for me," she continued. "I could have taken care of myself, but I just thought you might want some lunch."

"I'm glad you did. Time got away from me. So how was your television experience? What have you watched this morning?"

"I'd like to tell you I watched something highly educational, but I started watching the *Housewives* of something and immediately got hooked. The women are beautiful, but I've never seen such wasteful wealth. They fight about the most ridiculous things, but once I started watching, I couldn't look away."

He laughed and then sobered. "If you had their wealth, what would you do with it?"

She took a bite of her sandwich and chewed thoughtfully. "The first thing I would do is help all my friends in the swamp," she said after she swallowed. "I'd make sure all of them had good generators and cars. From what I see, you seem pretty well-off. What do you do with your excess money?" She flushed then. "I'm sorry, that is completely not my business and out of line."

"No, it's okay," he replied, not offended by her question at all. "I am pretty well-off, thanks to a trust fund and an inheritance from my grandfather. I'm incredibly lucky, and I try to give back in several ways. I defend many clients from the swamp pro bono. I also give generously to a couple of charities. The first one is a no-kill shelter for dogs and the second one is cancer. I lost my grandfather to pancreatic cancer, and I know you lost your father to cancer as well."

She nodded, the movement swinging her long, beautiful hair. "Were you close with your grandfather?" she asked.

"Very. He was the one person in my life who was al-

ways there for me, the person I could count on no matter what. He was my biggest champion." Talking about
him brought forth a grief Nick rarely allowed himself
to visit. Even after all the years that had passed, Nick
still missed the old man terribly.

"How old were you when he passed?" she asked
softly, her big, doe-like eyes filled with sympathy.

"I was fourteen, and when he died it felt as if the very
center of my world exploded, leaving me with nothing."
He released a short laugh. "This lunch talk has gotten
way too deep and heavy. Now, tell me more about these
housewives you've been watching."

For the next half hour as they ate, she regaled him
with the antics of five beautiful, wealthy women. He
loved to watch her as she spoke. Her features became
so animated, reflecting all her emotions, and he enjoyed
every minute of it.

With each conversation he had with her, he felt more
and more drawn to her not just physically, but emotionally as well. She was so open and warm.

But he wasn't about to allow himself to experience
another Delia situation. No matter what happened between him and Heather, he intended to closely guard
his heart.

After lunch, they watched a movie he thought she
would enjoy. The romantic comedy made her laugh,
which was exactly what he'd wanted it to do. The fact
that she'd been through so much and still had her laughter was awe-inspiring to him.

"Maybe you should take a little nap," he suggested

when the movie was over. "We'll plan our surveillance tonight between ten and two. Is that okay?"

There was no laughter in her eyes now as she gazed at him solemnly. "I guess tonight is as good as any night to start. The faster we identify this guy and prove he's the killer, the faster I'll be out of your house."

He realized he wasn't ready for her to get out of his house too quickly. So far, he was enjoying her company. His house…he had needed her energy and the conversation to battle the loneliness he'd felt when he was home alone.

She went to her room to nap, and he sat in the living room, realizing that he was a little tired himself. Last night, when he'd gotten the call from Etienne telling him that several men had broken into Heather's shanty, he'd immediately jumped out of bed, dressed and got on the road to get to her.

He'd been terrified of what they might find at her house. Had the men somehow assaulted her? Was she hurt…or worse? Guilt had ridden like a glowering passenger in his car. He'd been so sure she'd be safe there. Hell, he'd encouraged her to stay at the shanty.

The wild emotions, coupled with the time spent up in the middle of the night, now caught up with him. He leaned his head back and closed his eyes. His last thought was that having Heather here was a definite temptation, one he was determined to fight against.

Chapter Nine

The next four days passed fairly quickly as Heather and Nick fell into a comfortable routine. He cooked breakfast for them in the mornings, and she cooked them dinner every night. Then late at night, she, Nick and Bruno would sit in front of the drug house watching for the man she was desperate to identify, but so far, no luck.

Tonight, it would be only her and Nick on surveillance. Since it was Saturday night, Bruno was headed back to the Voodoo Lounge to question more people about the night Wesley had been murdered. Hopefully, he would find some answers for them, answers that would help exonerate her of the charges against her.

Nick. Being around him had become an exquisite form of torture for her. As they had more conversations and got to know each other on a deeper level, her desire for him grew.

All she'd been able to think about was the kiss they had shared and how much she wanted him to kiss her again. There had been moments when she'd thought he was going to, but each time he quickly distanced himself instead.

It was just before ten when she changed the blouse

she'd worn all day and pulled on a black tank top. It got quite warm at night sitting in the car without the air conditioning on.

She left her bedroom, and Nick was waiting for her in the living room. "Ready to go play detective again?" he asked.

He was clad in a pair of dark jeans with a black T-shirt, and his shoulder holster and gun were his only accessories. He looked slightly dangerous and incredibly hot.

"As ready as I can be," she replied.

A few minutes later, they left his garage. "First stop…our favorite convenience store," he said as he drove out of his driveway.

Each night, they stopped at the same convenience store to get drinks and snacks for the time they'd be sitting idly in the car. He pulled up in front of the store, parked and looked around.

"Okay, let's go get our goodies," he said as he unfastened his seat belt.

"I'll just wait out here. You know what I like," she replied. They bought the same items every night, so there was really no reason for her to go in with him.

"I'll be right back." He got out of the car and went inside the store, leaving behind the attractive scent of his cologne.

She looked around the area. There was only one other car in the parking lot, and that held a bunch of laughing teenage boys who she felt no threat from. However, there had been several times over the last few days when she'd felt like somebody was watching

them. Nick had assured her she was just being para-
noid, which he certainly understood.

Still, she felt as if she was holding her breath, just
waiting for danger to find her again, and this time she
was scared to death she wouldn't be so lucky.

Nick came back to the car, carrying a drink holder
with two sodas and a plastic bag filled with snacks. "I
got the cheddar chips that we both like. I got your lic-
orice and cinnamon bears, and I got the usual peanut
candy bars and butterscotch disks for me."

"Then we should be all set for another four hours of
surveillance and snacking," she replied.

"I think the kid behind the counter believes we're
pot smokers and we get the munchies around this time
each night," he said with humor as he handed her the
drinks and the bag and then started the car.

"Oh, lordy, that's all I need, a rumor going around
that I murder men and do drugs," she replied.

He laughed. "Don't worry too much about it. I have a
feeling nobody would believe the kid anyway. Besides,
what's a little pot smoking rumor when you're facing
a murder charge."

"True," she replied. "Have you ever smoked it before?" she asked curiously as he drove out of the store's
parking lot and onto the main road again.

"I tried it years ago, but it wasn't my thing. I don't
like not feeling in complete control, so drugs just aren't
in my life." He flashed her a quick glance. "What about
you? Have you ever tried anything?"

"No. I've never had the desire to try any kind of

drugs," she replied. "Although, I could become quite addicted to cinnamon bears."

He laughed once again. She loved the sound of his laughter. It was deep and rich and a sheer pleasure to hear. They then rode for a few minutes in a comfortable silence.

When they were just down the street from the drug house, he parked against the curb. They were close enough that from this vantage point they would be able to see who came and went from the house. The rundown place was definitely a blight to the nicer homes on the block.

"So, what deep topic are we going to delve into tonight to pass the time?" she asked once they were settled in. The drinks were in the holders between them, and the bag was in her lap.

He reached over and pulled out the cheddar-flavored potato chips. He ripped open the top of the bag and then held it out to her. "I was thinking maybe we needed to have a conversation about space aliens."

She laughed and grabbed a handful of the chips. "Okay, then space aliens it is."

"Do you believe in them?"

"I believe it is foolish for us to believe that we are the only people in the entire universe, so yes I do believe in them," she replied. "What about you?"

"I'm a believer. Do you think aliens are here on earth and walk among us?"

"No, I don't believe that," she replied. "Do you?"

"I don't know, I've definitely met a few people in town I'd consider real space cadets," he said.

She laughed. "I think that's different than space aliens. I imagine aliens would have to be highly intelligent to be here and conceal themselves among us."

"Do you think they're around with evil intent in their hearts? Do you think they're just waiting for the perfect moment to take over our world and then eat us as snacks?"

"I think that's a lot of hogwash. If they wanted to take over, they would have done it by now." She crunched on a couple of chips and then took a drink from her soda. "I don't lose any sleep worrying about an imminent alien invasion," she added.

"I sleep with an aluminum hat on every night so the aliens don't get in my head," he replied.

She laughed once again at the mental image of the very hot man with a silly aluminum hat on his head. "Does it have antennas, too?"

"Nah, I was afraid antennas would somehow call them to me," he replied.

"I'd like to see you in your hat sometime."

He grinned at her, his handsome features visible in the illumination from a nearby streetlight. "It's a very special thing for me to share. In fact, I've never shared it with anyone before."

He stopped talking as a car pulled into the driveway of the house and two men got out. Heather looked at them from the moment they left the car until they disappeared into the house.

"Neither of them is the man I remember arguing with Wesley," she finally said dispiritedly.

"That's okay. If he's in the drug trade, then hopefully he'll eventually show up here, and we'll be able to identify him," Nick replied.

"The trial date is coming closer and closer. What happens if I don't see this guy again? And just because he had a fight with Wesley, that doesn't necessarily mean he killed him." A deep anxiety tightened her stomach muscles, and she began to chew on her index fingernail.

He reached out and pulled her hand away from her mouth. "If you continue to chew on that nail, you're eventually going to eat your whole finger."

"I know, it's a terrible habit. I only do it when I'm really anxious."

"Well, don't be really anxious. Even if we don't identify this man, even if we don't catch the killer, I've been working on a strong defense for you. I've got you covered. I've got you, Heather."

It was impossible to hang on to the anxiety when his blue eyes gazed into hers so earnestly, when his simplest touch eased the jumping nerves inside her and his voice rang with such authority and confidence.

They'd only shared a single kiss, but she found herself falling hard for him. For the past four days, they had essentially been living like husband and wife, except they didn't share a bedroom.

She looked forward to seeing him first thing in the morning, and she liked the fact that he was the last person she saw before she went to sleep. He often worked in his home office in the afternoons while she sat in the living room and watched television. Then they came back together for dinner.

It had become a comfortable routine although she missed her plants and her work. Lucy was opening the shop in her spare time and was taking care of watering the plants. While Heather appreciated that Lucy was trying to help her, she didn't even know what half the plants were.

Still, Heather wasn't used to having so much idle time. It gave her time to worry about what was to become of her. Would her life ever go back to what it had been before? Did Nick really have a strong defense? Would he tell her if he didn't?

Her thoughts were interrupted as another car pulled up in front of the house and two new men got out and went inside. Neither of them was the person Heather most wanted to see.

"Busy night at the drug house," Nick observed as the previous two cars left and another car pulled in, this one containing a young, thin woman. "A shipment must have come in. I'm surprised Etienne doesn't have some men out here watching the house or making some arrests."

"I'm sure all of his officers are tied up with the Swamp Soul Stealer's latest case," she replied.

"Yeah. It's too bad our police department isn't bigger so the police could be everywhere," he said. "But I know Etienne is doing the best he can with what manpower he has."

"Maybe it's time he gets a bigger budget," she replied. "Then he could hire more men."

"That needs to be brought up at the next town council meeting," he replied. "I'll make sure it is. I think it's been a while since we voted on more money for the police department."

Their conversation changed to all things strange and unusual. They talked about Bigfoot and the Loch Ness Monster. They broke into their candy stash, and she chewed the little cinnamon bears while he ate a peanut bar and then some of his butterscotch disks.

There was something intimate about two people sitting in a car in the middle of the night and talking about anything and everything that came to their minds.

There was a lull in the traffic for a little while, and then all of a sudden, the front door flew open and a man strode outside. He was a big guy, and he wore a shoulder holster and carried a big flashlight.

A new anxiety filled her as he began checking the vehicles parked along the curb. "Nick, you need to drive away," she said urgently. "He's going to see us. He's going to catch us."

"I can't drive off now. It would be too obvious. Just follow my lead."

When the man approached the side of their car, Nick reached over and pulled her half over the console. He wrapped his arms around her and then took her lips with his.

Despite the fact that she was terrified, she couldn't help the flames of desire that were lit inside her by the unexpected deep kiss. She clung to his shoulders and prayed the man would pass them by.

Even though she had her eyes closed, a flash of light penetrated her eyelids, and she knew the man was shining his flashlight into the car.

Nick tightened his arms around her, and through his half-opened window, she heard the man chuckle and then sensed he moved on. Nick continued to kiss her for several long minutes. The kiss tasted of a heated desire and sweet butterscotch.

He finally released her, and she quickly looked outside and saw the man now on the opposite side of the street and heading back toward the house.

"That was a close call," Nick said.

"Far too close for me," she replied and fought the impulse to chew on her nail as a wave of anxiety swept through her. Even though the kiss had been very hot, the circumstances that had prompted it had been terrifying.

"I would assume he was looking for any cops who might be parked in the area and watching the place." Nick grabbed another candy bar from the bag on her lap and grinned at her. "Kissing you was a very hot way to avoid danger."

"I agree," she replied as the warmth of a blush filled her cheeks.

"He probably thought we belonged in one of the houses or were in the car because we are in the middle of a passionate affair."

"I'm just grateful the kiss worked, and he left us alone," she replied.

One thing was for sure, the kiss had confirmed to her that she was definitely falling in love with her defense attorney.

She now not only hoped that he would save her from going to prison for years, but also that he could save her heart by loving her back.

THE KISS WITH Heather had ignited an intense desire for her despite the circumstances surrounding the kiss. In that moment, she had tasted of hot desire and sweet cinnamon, and he'd wanted to take advantage of the situation and continue kissing her, but he hadn't.

The next day, Nick sat in his office in town knowing Heather was safe at his house with Bruno there to guard over things. Even though it was late Sunday afternoon, he had a client who should be coming in at any moment, but instead of focusing on that case, it was thoughts of Heather that filled his head.

Living with her for the past five days had been sheer torture. He wanted to take her to his bed so badly. His desire for her ached in his veins and half dizzied his head whenever he was near her.

The last time he'd felt like this about a woman, the end results had been disastrous, and he'd wound up with a very broken heart. Of course, he wasn't about to let that happen a second time. He was positive he could make love with Heather and not be in love with her. He just had to make sure if that happened, she was on the same page.

There was a knock on his door, and Sharon poked her head in. "Mr. Raymore is here."

"Send him on in," Nick said.

Michael Raymore was sixty-three years old. He was overweight and going bald, and this was the second time he'd been arrested for shoplifting from one of the higher-end stores in town. His defense this time was he had every intention of paying for the two bottles of expensive cologne that were in his pockets at the time he was arrested just outside the store.

Nick had needed to meet Michael in person and get the appropriate papers signed to defend the man. It was a relatively easy case, and the best Nick was hoping for was to get the man probation and a fine instead of any jail time.

"I'm on disability," Michael whined. "And I'm all alone and looking for a wife. A man has to smell good when he's meeting the ladies. But I intended to pay for the cologne. I just forgot they were in my pockets when I walked out of the store."

It would have been much easier to have a little sympathy if the man had stolen food, but that wasn't the case. The whole appointment only lasted thirty minutes, and then Michael left and Sharon came back into Nick's office. "Do you need me for anything else?" she asked.

"No, but I want to thank you for coming in on a Sunday," he said.

She grinned at him. "You can thank me when you write out my next paycheck."

He laughed. "You got it."

The minute Sharon was gone, he got ready to leave as well. Heather would probably be in the kitchen, preparing dinner. He hadn't asked her to take care of the evening meals, but she had insisted she take over that task as part of her payment to him. He had to admit it was a real treat for him, and each night the meals so far had been delicious. The cook-off they had planned had gone by the wayside when she'd moved in with him.

He wondered how she and Bruno were getting along.

During the nights of their surveillance together, Bruno had barely spoken to her. He hadn't been blatantly rude, but he'd definitely been rather cool to her. Not that it mattered. Heather was only a temporary pleasure in Nick's life. Within weeks, hopefully Heather would be back to her life, and he'd be back hanging out with Bruno and living his own.

He had to admit, he was going to miss her when she was gone. The thought surprised him. He would miss the sound of her musical laughter ringing in the air. He would miss her company in the evenings when they talked about all kinds of things. She was witty and intelligent, and he enjoyed all their conversations.

By the time he pulled into his garage, he'd shoved all those thoughts to the back of his brain. He parked his car, closed the garage door behind him and then entered into the kitchen.

The room was empty, and the air was redolent with the scents of cooking chicken. He left the kitchen and went into the living room, where Bruno sat watching television.

"Where's Heather?" Nick asked.

"Back in her bedroom. I think she's on the phone talking to one of her friends," Bruno replied.

Nick sank down on the love seat. "How did it go while I was gone?"

Bruno shrugged. "Fine. She's mostly been in the kitchen. She invited me to stay for dinner, but I declined."

"Why? You know you would have been welcomed."

"I know, but actually I have a dinner date," Bruno replied.

"Really? With who?" Nick asked curiously.

Bruno appeared to squirm slightly. "Uh… Sharon."

Nick looked at his friend in surprise. "My Sharon?"

Bruno grinned. "She's not your Sharon, but yeah. It's no big deal. We're just going to the café to eat."

"When did this all come about?" Nick asked, still surprised.

"On Friday I was just talking with her, and I thought it would be nice to take her out to dinner."

"She was just at the office with me, and she didn't mention anything about it."

"Yeah, well we didn't know for sure how you would react."

At that moment, Heather came into the room. As always, she looked stunning even though she was dressed casually in a worn pair of jeans and a coral-colored T-shirt. The coral color looked amazing against her slightly olive coloring. She smiled at him. "Hi, I didn't realize you were home."

"I'm home."

She laughed. "I can see that. Dinner will be ready in about thirty minutes or so."

"Something definitely smells delicious," he said.

"It's a cheesy chicken-and-rice casserole. I found the recipe online," she replied.

"Sounds good to me," he said.

"I hope it is. I asked Bruno to stay for dinner, but he said he had other plans."

"Yeah, he just told me that," Nick replied.

"Now, I'll just be in the kitchen, and I'll let you know when it's ready."

She left the room, but not before he smelled the scent of her evocative perfume. He turned to look back at Bruno, who was staring at him. "What?"

"Are you getting in too deep with her?" Bruno asked softly.

"Not at all," Nick replied quickly. "She's just a client who happens to be staying here with me temporarily."

Bruno stared at him for another long minute and then released a deep sigh. "I just don't want to go through it with you again. I had to pick you up off the floor after Delia, and you weren't yourself for months after that."

"This is nothing like that," Nick protested. "Trust me, my heart isn't in any danger. I like Heather, and I'm enjoying her company, but that's it," he assured his friend.

"Okay then." Bruno rose to his feet. "I'm going to head out of here. I need to change and get ready for my date."

"Thanks for today, and I hope you have a good time with Sharon," Nick said. "Just don't break her heart."

"Right," Bruno replied dryly. "Because I've always been such a heartbreaker."

Once he was gone, Nick went into the kitchen, where Heather was stirring something on the stove top. "Can I help you with anything?" he asked.

"No, just have a seat and relax," she replied. "Are you hungry?"

"Yeah, I am. I wasn't until I walked into the house and smelled dinner," he replied. The table was already set with two plates and the appropriate silverware.

He sat in the chair he always sat in to eat and watched

her. She moved with a gracefulness that was attractive. "So, how was your appointment?" She moved a saucepan from the burner and then turned and looked at him.

"The appointment went fine. My newest client is a shoplifter, and Tommy Radcliffe is throwing the book at him for having two colognes in his possession that he didn't pay for when he walked out of the store."

"Your job will be to get him a lighter sentence?"

"That's it. How was your time with Bruno while I was gone?"

A small frown danced into the center of her forehead. "It was fine. I still get the feeling that he doesn't like me."

"I told you before, he's a cautious kind of guy," Nick replied.

"What does he think I'm going to do?"

He's afraid you'll steal my heart and then dump me. The thought remained in his head and wasn't spoken aloud. "I don't know, but he'll eventually come around."

"I hope so." She went to the oven and used mitts to take out a covered casserole dish. She set it on an awaiting hot pad in the center of the table. She then moved carrots from the saucepan to a serving bowl. Finally, she got from the refrigerator a fresh green salad and a bottle of ranch dressing.

She took the foil off the casserole dish to expose a bed of rice with several chicken breasts on top. "This all looks amazing," he said.

"Let's hope it tastes as good as it looks," she replied as she sank down in the chair opposite him.

"You are a very good cook," he said minutes later as he ate the food she'd prepared.

"I'm enjoying the novelty of having an oven," she replied.

"Do you miss your shanty?"

She nodded, her long hair gleaming richly beneath the light over the table. "I talked to Lucy for a while today, and it made me a little homesick. I'm also worried about all my plants. Lucy is watering the ones at my house and at the shop, but despite her good intentions, she really doesn't know what she's doing."

"If you want, we can go to the shop tomorrow, and you can check things out." He saw the look of trepidation that immediately crossed her features.

"The last time we were at the shop things didn't go so well for us," she said.

"This time we'll take Bruno with us, and we'll be well prepared for anything." Nick smiled at her. "I got you," he said in an effort to ease her mind.

"And I appreciate that," she replied.

As they finished up the meal, they talked about past cases he'd had and some of the customers that frequented her shop. He helped her with the cleanup, and each time he inadvertently touched her, a tormenting desire shot through his veins.

By the time they sat side by side on the sofa to watch a movie, he felt as if he were on fire with his want of her. Apparently, she didn't pick up on his mood, but each unconscious movement she made only shot his desire even higher.

When she flipped strands of her dark, luxurious hair

over her shoulder, it felt like an open invitation for him to wrap his fingers in it and pull her close. Every time she changed positions, a new waft of her scent filled his head.

He could scarcely pay attention to the movie as he was so captivated by her closeness to him. However, when a sad part of the movie played, he saw the spark of tears in her eyes.

"Hey, are you crying?" he asked and threw an arm around her shoulder.

She sniffled and released an embarrassed laugh. "That part was so sad," she replied and leaned into him. "Silly of me to cry over a movie."

"I don't find it silly at all," he said and pulled her closer into his side. "In fact, I find it quite charming."

She looked up at him and her eyes no longer held sadness, but rather an invitation, and at the same time her lips parted slightly.

He took the invitation by capturing her mouth with his. She immediately wrapped her arms around his neck and leaned closer to him. Her lips were incredibly pillowy, and when she opened them fully to him, his tongue danced in to swirl with hers. Just that quickly, he was completely lost in her.

He tangled his hands in her long, silky hair and continued the kiss until they were both breathless and panting. "Heather, I really want to make love to you," he finally said as the kiss ended.

"And I really want to make love to you," she replied, her eyes smoldering with unmistakable desire.

He stood and held out his hand to her. She hesitated

only a moment and then slipped her hand into his. "But before we do this, I need you to understand I'm not promising you anything beyond this moment."

"I'm not expecting anything more than that from you," she replied half breathlessly.

She rose from the sofa, and together they headed down the hall to his bedroom. His heart beat a rhythm of excitement, and his blood rushed hot through his veins. Surely after this one time of letting go of self-control, she'd be out of his system for good, and they would go back to a strictly client-and-lawyer relationship.

Chapter Ten

Heather got a quick glimpse of his large, beautiful bedroom. It was as if she'd stepped into her deepest, most desired fantasy. Being in Nick's arms was beyond heavenly. She tasted his desire for her in his kiss, and as he drew her closer and closer, she felt his desire for her in his obvious arousal that pressed against her.

It had been years since she had felt a man's arms around her and tasted this kind of hot hunger. It was exhilarating…intoxicating, and she couldn't get enough of it.

Their kiss lasted until he ended it and stepped back from her. His blue eyes simmered with fiery flames as he unbuttoned his white shirt and shrugged it off his shoulders and to the floor behind him.

Oh, a half-naked Nick was positively splendid. His broad chest was well muscled and gleamed in the twilight illumination coming through the nearby window. His chest tapered to a slim but muscular abdomen.

She reached out and ran her hands down his smooth, warm skin and then followed her hands with her mouth. She slid kisses down his chest for only a moment before he pulled her back into his arms for another long, breath-stealing kiss.

This time as he kissed her, he tugged the bottom of her T-shirt out of her jeans, and ended the kiss as he slid the garment up and over her head.

"Heather, you are so beautiful," he whispered as she stood before him in her lacy light pink bra.

"Thank you," she replied. Oh, she was ready for so much more. She wanted to be naked for him…with him. She wanted to feel her naked body intimately close against his own.

As he unfastened the top of his slacks, she unbuttoned the fly of her jeans. Once it was unbuttoned, she pushed them down and then off. By that time, he was only clad in his black boxers, and she was in a pair of lacy pink panties. He reached over and pulled down the top of the black bedspread, exposing white sheets and an invitation for her to get into the bed.

She slid into the sheets, and he followed her and then immediately pulled her into his arms once again. His bare skin met hers, and she thrilled at the way his warm body felt so close to her.

They kissed hungrily, their tongues swirling together and whipping their desire for each other higher and higher. She moved her hips against his, and he reached behind her and unfastened her bra. He plucked it off her and tossed it to the foot of the bed. She gasped in pleasure as his hands captured her breasts. His palms were so warm against them. He then rolled his thumb across her erect nipples, shooting pleasure from the throbbing tips to the very center of her. The pleasure only increased when his tongue flicked and toyed where his fingers had been.

She was lost in him…in the mindless pleasure that torched through her at his every touch. His scent surrounded her, the wonderful fragrance that spoke of safety and caring. She moaned with delight as his hands slowly moved down the length of her body and stopped at the waistband of her panties.

She wanted them off, and she wanted his boxers off, too. She was more than ready to be completely naked with him. He pulled her panties down far enough that she could kick them off.

Once she was naked, she moved her hands to the top of his boxers. "Take them off, Nick. I want you to be completely naked with me," she whispered breathlessly.

He immediately complied and then pulled her back into his arms and kissed her long and deep. Her body was now intimately close to his, and he was fully aroused. The kiss ended and his hands once again slid down the length of her body to the very center of her.

She gasped as his fingers began to dance against her sensitive skin and created a rising tension inside her. Higher and higher she climbed until she crashed down to the earth with a fierce orgasm. She cried out his name and clung to him until the exquisite moment finally ended.

But it still wasn't enough for her. She wanted more of him. She reached down and took his erection in her hand. It was hard, yet the skin covering it was velvety soft. He groaned as she moved her hand up and down in slow, even strokes. His erection grew even harder and bigger.

"Heather, I want you so badly," he said, his voice deeper than normal.

"Then take me, Nick," she gasped breathlessly. "Take me now."

She pulled her hand away from him, and he positioned himself between her open thighs. In the final light of day drifting through the window, his simmering blue gaze held hers for a long moment.

He slowly eased into her, filling her up as she once again gasped his name. For a long moment, he didn't move and then he began to pump into her, slowly at first and then faster and faster. She clung to his shoulders, meeting him thrust for thrust.

A new rising tension built inside her. Higher and higher she rode the waves of intense pleasure until she crested and shuddered with another powerful orgasm.

At the same time with a groan of her name, he found his own release. For several long moments, they remained locked together as they tried to catch their breaths.

Finally, he leaned down and captured her lips in a tender kiss. He ended the kiss and then rolled over to the side of her. "Wow," he said.

She laughed joyously. "Wow is right."

He leaned up on one elbow and gazed down at her with a frown. "That all happened so fast, we didn't even think about birth control."

"It's okay, I'm on the pill, and I haven't been with

anyone for years, so you don't have to worry about anything else with me," she replied.

"And it's been well over a year since I've been with anyone," he replied, his frown gone.

"Really? I would think a successful man who looks like you could have a different woman every single night of the week," she replied.

He released a small laugh and then quickly sobered. "Well, I don't know about all that, but I quit dating a little over a year ago. When I was much younger, I had the dream of a wife and a couple of children, but I came to the conclusion that I'm better off all alone."

"But, Nick, that's so sad," she replied. He was such a kind, thoughtful man. She was sure he would make a wonderful husband and father.

"I guess you still have a dream of that one special man…marriage and eventually a couple of kids," he replied.

"Definitely, that's exactly what I want."

"Then I hope that's what's in your future." He leaned over and kissed her on the cheek then rolled out of the bed. "You can use my bathroom. I'll use the one in the hallway." He grabbed his boxers from the floor and then left the room.

She immediately got out of the bed and gathered up all her clothes and then went into the adjoining bathroom. The decor there was black and gold. His shower was big enough to accommodate several people at the same time and had four sprays coming out of the walls.

She could only imagine such luxury. When she showered, she only got a trickling spray of water, and it didn't last long. She cleaned up and got dressed. Her body was still warm in the aftermath of what they had shared, and her emotions were all over the place.

If she had believed herself to be falling for Nick, then the fall was now complete. She was in love with him, not that it mattered. He was obviously in a different headspace than she was. She was just a client who he happened to desire, and she'd do well to remember that.

She would have loved to spend the night in his arms. She would have loved to fall asleep with him spooned around her and with his warm breath caressing the back of her neck. But he wasn't inviting her to spend the night in his bed. Her heart squeezed tight with a sharp pain as her love for him buoyed up inside her. It was a love he obviously didn't feel for her and it was that thought that hurt her heart.

Once she was dressed, she went back into the bedroom. Nick wasn't there, so she went into the living room and sank down on the sofa. Minutes later, he joined her. He sat next to her on the sofa and pulled her close against him.

"Heather, I just want you to know that I consider what we just shared very special," he said. His eyes were warm and caring as he gazed at her.

Her heart constricted once again. "It was very special to me, too."

"But you do realize it should never have happened and shouldn't happen again. I would never want to take advantage of your vulnerability, considering our positions."

"Oh, Nick, you didn't...you couldn't take advantage

of me. I wanted you, and it was as simple as that, and you obviously wanted me, too," she replied. "We are two consenting adults, and I wouldn't take back a minute of what we just shared."

"Still, it shouldn't happen again," he replied firmly.

"I'm not sure why, but okay. And I think on that note, I'll head to bed. These late nights of surveillance have finally caught up with me, and I'm really tired."

"I hear that," he replied and pulled his arm from around her. "I'm extra tired tonight myself, although the last of my energy was certainly well spent."

She laughed and stood. "Same. So, I'll just say goodnight now, and I'll see you in the morning."

"Goodnight, Heather," he replied.

"'Night, Nick." She left the living room and went into her bedroom. From there, she immediately beelined to the bathroom and started running the water for a bath. Next to the tub was a pretty container that held lavender-scented bath salts and a bottle of lavender bubble bath.

She sprinkled a little of both into the water, and then once the tub was full, she stripped naked and slid into the hot, scented water.

It felt absolutely heavenly. She leaned her head back and closed her eyes and thought about everything that had happened. No matter what, she would never, ever regret making love with Nick.

The whole experience had been beyond wonderful. Even though she had relatively little sexual experience, she knew he'd been a particularly caring partner. He'd taken her to heights of pleasure she'd never even known existed before.

If things went really badly for her and Nick couldn't keep her out of prison, then at least she would have this single memory to warm her heart on lonely, frightening nights behind bars.

MAKING LOVE WITH Heather had been even better than in his wildest imagination. She'd been so passionate, and her passion had fed his even higher than it had been. He'd thought having her once would get her out of his system, but the moment it was over, he wanted her all over again.

This morning, he'd awakened much earlier than usual and now sat at the kitchen table sipping a cup of coffee and thinking about his lovely houseguest.

There was no question he'd been developing feelings for her…deep feelings that were dangerous for him to have. Even if he fell in love with her and she professed to feel the same way toward him, he would never know if her love was real and not based in a wealth of gratitude. He still thought it was very possible that if he got her off the charges against her, she would walk out of his life without a backward glance.

It was definitely time he began to distance himself from her and maintain a more professional relationship with her. Thinking about the case against her made his stomach tighten with anxiety.

They still had nothing to take to Etienne to make him reinvestigate the case, and he still had no real evidence to show to a jury that she had been set up.

Jury selection started in less than three weeks. He had to make sure nobody with any prejudices toward people from the swamp was sitting on the jury.

Tommy Radcliffe had an easy tale to tell about the beautiful, poor swamp woman who had an affair with the wealthy, married Wesley. He would play up the fiction that Heather desperately wanted out of the swamp and Wesley was her ticket out. He'd make Wesley look like a choir boy whose only fault was being weak and unable to fight against Heather's wiles. Nick's fear was it was a tale that was far too easily believed.

He could argue she was too petite to kill the much bigger man, and Tommy would argue that anger and rage had given her the necessary strength to act in a murderous frenzy.

Nick could also argue the drug connection, but without any real evidence to back it up, it probably wouldn't fly. Although he would never tell Heather, the truth of the matter was Nick was worried.

He'd just poured himself a second cup of coffee when Heather came into the kitchen. Clad in a pair of jeans and a blue sleeveless blouse, and with her hair loose around her shoulders, she looked positively gorgeous. A lot of her beauty came from the fact that she didn't seem aware of just how pretty she was.

"Good morning," he greeted her.

She smiled. "Back at you," she replied as she headed toward the coffee.

"How did you sleep?"

"Like a baby," she said.

"I was thinking pancakes this morning."

She grinned again. "I like the way you think." She poured her coffee and then joined him at the table. "How did you sleep?"

"I slept fine. Are you hungry?"

"I'm starving," she admitted.

"You like sausage?"

"I do."

"Then sausage and pancakes it is." He got up from the table and began to work on breakfast. He was grateful that their conversation remained light and easy. He was particularly glad that there was no awkward rehash of what had happened between them the night before.

It didn't take him long to have a platter of sausage and a stack of pancakes ready. He placed both on the table and then added butter and warmed-up maple syrup.

"Eating pancakes is kind of like having dessert in the morning," she said after they started eating. "And you make a great pancake."

"Thanks. I could eat pancakes or French toast almost every day for breakfast," he replied.

"It's the maple syrup sweetness," she said.

A drop of the syrup clung to her lower lip, and he wanted nothing more than to lean across the table and cover her sweet-tasting mouth with his. Damn, this all would be so much easier if he had no desire for her, if he didn't like her so damned much.

They had just finished eating when a knock fell on his front door. "I'll be right back." He got up from the table, grabbed his gun from the nearby counter and then went to answer.

It was Bruno. "Why didn't you just let yourself in?" Nick asked. "You have a key, and you've always let yourself in before."

"You know I don't like to do that," Bruno replied. "Especially now since you have a woman living here with you."

"What do you expect? To walk in and see her sitting on the sofa naked?" Nick replied in amusement.

"Don't give me a hard time, bro. I haven't even had my coffee this morning. Besides, I come with news."

Nick raised a brow curiously. "Good news?"

"Give me a cup of coffee, and I'll tell you all."

"Come on in. Heather and I were just finishing up breakfast." Nick led his friend into the kitchen.

"Good morning, Bruno," Heather said.

"Good morning to you," he replied and beelined to the coffee maker.

Nick returned to his chair at the table. "You want some pancakes?"

"Nah, I'm good." Bruno poured himself a cup of coffee and then joined them at the table. "You guys go ahead and eat, and I'll do the talking."

"We're finished eating, so talk," Nick said.

"Okay, as you know, last night I took Sharon to the café for dinner," Bruno began.

"Oh, that's nice," Heather said. "She seems like a wonderful woman."

"How did things go between the two of you?" Nick asked.

A hint of a smile lifted a corner of Bruno's mouth. "I enjoyed it, and I think she did, too. Anyway, after dinner we decided to go to the Voodoo Lounge and have a drink. We sat at the bar because we didn't intend to be there that long."

He paused and took a drink of his coffee. Nick fought the urge to hurry the man along and get to the point. Bruno said he had news, but Nick still didn't know if it was good news and something that might help Heather's case or bad news that would hurt her.

"Anyway," Bruno continued, "we were sitting at the bar, and we got to visiting with a couple who was sitting next to us. The conversation went to the night of the murder, and they told me they were there that night and they saw Heather being helped out the back door by a squat, dark-haired man."

"Finally, witnesses we can use," Nick exclaimed with excitement.

"Thank God," Heather said tremulously.

"Slow down, I haven't finished yet," Bruno said. "I asked them if they'd told the cops what they saw concerning Heather, and they told me that they hadn't because they didn't want to get involved. When I asked for their names, they declined to give them to me and left soon after that."

"So, we don't have their names," Nick said as a deep disappointment slammed into his chest.

"Oh, boss of little faith," Bruno replied with a full grin. He pulled a small notepad from his T-shirt pocket. "The bartender was more than happy to tell me that Sharon and I were visiting with regulars Paul and Anette Darnel." He handed Nick a page from the notebook with the names written on it.

"I've always said you're the best," Nick said to his friend.

"But if they don't want to get involved, then what good are they?" Heather said softly. "I mean, apparently they were ready to let an innocent woman go to jail."

Nick frowned. "We'll take this information to Etienne and see if this is enough for him to reopen the case. I'll also subpoena them, and they will have to talk at trial. Good work, Bruno."

"Thank you for working so hard on my behalf," Heather said.

"No problem," Bruno replied.

"Let's talk about the plans for the day," Nick said, still excited at the prospect of having witnesses that worked in his defense case.

"What's the plan?" Bruno asked.

"The first thing we'll do is have a little chat with Etienne, and after that Heather needs to go to her store to water some of the plants there. I would like you to go with us."

"My time is yours," Bruno replied.

Nick leaned over and grabbed one of Heather's hands in his. "This is the first real break we've gotten in the case." He grinned at her, squeezed her hand and then released it.

"I'm afraid to get too excited for fear I'll just be let down," she replied.

"I'm hoping to find more people to substantiate the fact that the killer took you out the back door," Bruno said. "If there were two who saw that, then there are probably ten. It's just a matter of me finding them and getting their names."

"Why would nobody come forward to tell the police that? Why not tell the police the next morning after they heard I'd been arrested for the murder?" Heather asked.

"My guess is that the guy who took you outside that night looked like a real bad guy. The witnesses who saw him might have been afraid of retribution if they came forward."

"What a sad state of society it is," Heather said with a shake of her head.

"It's the times we live in," Nick replied. "Good people are afraid to get involved with anything crime related. It's how women get beat up in a public place and nobody steps up to stop it."

"I would hope the people of Crystal Cove were different," Heather said.

"People are people no matter where they live," Bruno replied.

"Let's get the kitchen cleaned up so we can get on our way," Nick said as he stood. "Bruno, feel free to help yourself to another cup of coffee."

Heather helped with the cleanup, and within twenty minutes they were all ready to go. Bruno sat in the passenger seat of Nick's car, and Heather sat in the back seat. He knew his partner would be watching in all directions for any trouble approaching their car.

As Nick drove toward the police station, he hoped like hell this was enough to finally get the lawman to reinvestigate the case. If not that, then he hoped Etienne would talk to Tommy Radcliffe about dropping the case against Heather.

It was a matter of justice, and as prosecuting attor-

ney, Tommy should want to see real justice done. Now
that they had witnesses to corroborate Heather's story,
Tommy should want to do the right thing and get the
real killer behind bars. And that wasn't Heather.

However, Tommy had always been a bit of a grand-
stander, and this was the case he'd been yearning for—
it had garnered a lot of publicity, and he would probably
be playing to a full house of people attending the trial.

When they reached the police station, Etienne was
in his office. "Let's make this quick," he said once they
were before him. "I just got word that another person
has disappeared in the swamp."

"Who?" Heather asked, obviously worried about her
friends there.

"Clayton Beauregarde," Etienne replied.

"Do you know him?" Nick asked Heather.

"Yes. His wife is Lillie, and they recently had their
first child," Heather replied, her dark eyes simmering
with sadness.

"According to Lillie, last night he left his place to
make a quick run to the grocery store. Unfortunately,
he never came home." A muscle ticked in Etienne's
tense jaw. "Now, what's up?"

Bruno explained about the couple he had met the
night before and how he had gotten their names from
the bartender. "They're witnesses to the fact that
Heather was half carried by a man out of the back door,"
Nick added. "This is proof that there was somebody
else in that alley the night that Wesley was murdered."

"Then use them as witnesses for your case," Etienne
said, obviously distracted by the crime at hand.

Nick knew he wasn't going to get anywhere with Etienne, at least not today with a new man missing from the swamp. "I know you're busy right now, so we'll get out of your hair. But maybe in a couple of days you can sit down with me for a talk."

"Great, now if you'll excuse me, I was just on my way out," Etienne said.

Within minutes, they were all back in the car and headed to Heather's shop. "I think you're on your own from here on out," Bruno said, voicing what Nick was thinking.

"What does that mean?" Heather asked.

"It means that we can't depend on Etienne to reinvestigate the case or do much of anything else. We'll just have to take our chances at trial," Nick replied. He looked in his rearview mirror. Heather was chewing on her nail, obviously apprehensive.

Nick hadn't realized just how much he'd hoped Etienne would immediately reinvestigate the case until now, when he feared that wasn't going to happen. Nick didn't blame Heather for being anxious. For the first time since he'd taken her case, he was really anxious, too.

Chapter Eleven

Another week passed and the closer her trial got, the more Heather worried about what was going to happen to her. Still, despite her concerns, spending time with Nick only made her feelings toward him deepen.

She awoke early on Sunday morning in Nick's bed. Apparently, he had awakened even earlier as she was alone in the bed that smelled of his cologne. Instead of getting up, she rolled over on her back and thought about the week that had passed.

Nick was spending more time in his home office working on her case, and Heather continued to cook their evening meal. Bruno had found two more people who had seen Heather being "helped" out of the back door by a rough-looking man. Unfortunately, like the first couple, these people also indicated they didn't want to get involved.

However, Nick had the names of the four people, and after finding out their addresses, he intended to seek subpoenas so they would have to testify for the defense.

"I got you," Nick kept telling her, and when she gazed into the depths of his beautiful blue eyes, she believed him. She also believed he was developing strong feelings for her. She felt it in his touch and saw it in his eyes when he gazed at her. There was a softness… a genuine caring there, and it warmed and excited her.

Then there had been last night. The two of them had gone on their surveillance duty while Bruno had gone to the bar. It had been another uneventful night, and when she and Nick had gotten home, they had shared a kiss. It was supposed to be a simple, good-night kiss. But it quickly became something much deeper, much hotter, and just that quickly they were out of control and had wound up in his bed.

She stretched, satisfied as a gator after eating a full meal. It had been Nick who had invited her to spend the night in his bed, and it had been beyond wonderful to fall asleep with him spooning closely around her and his arm around her waist and holding her tight.

Suddenly, she couldn't wait to see him. She got out of his bed, quickly made it and then went into her own bedroom to get dressed for the day.

By the time she left her bedroom, the scent of bacon and coffee wafted in the air. "Hmm, smells like breakfast," she said as she entered the kitchen.

Nick turned from the stove and grinned at her. "I figured that would get you out of bed."

She laughed. "You know I love your breakfasts."

"Almost as much as I love your dinners," he replied. "How about omelets this morning?"

"You know I especially love your omelets." She grinned at him and then poured herself a cup of coffee and sat down at the table. She watched him work, comfortable in the silence as he prepared the omelets.

He didn't speak again until he had breakfast on the table. As they ate, they talked about the latest on the Swamp Soul Stealer case. Clayton Beauregarde had yet to be found, although a bag of groceries had been found on the ground not far from his shanty.

"The heartbreaking thing is he was so close to being home…so close to being safe when he was taken," Heather said.

"Yeah, that makes it that much more disheartening," Nick agreed. "I'd like to know how he manages to disable these people so quickly. Nobody ever hears anything. No screams…no calls for help…nothing."

"I know Etienne has pinned a lot of his hopes on Colette Broussard waking up and being able to tell him who the monster is and where he's keeping all the people he kidnapped, but what if, God forbid, Colette never wakes up?"

Nick shrugged. "Who knows? I know Etienne is doing everything in his power to find this creep, but from what I hear, the creep isn't making any mistakes."

"If you were to guess, would you think it's somebody from town or somebody from the swamp?" she asked.

He frowned thoughtfully. "It would help if we knew the motive. There are days I think it has to be somebody from town who is prejudiced against the swamp people. Then there are other days I think that only somebody from the swamp could sneak around and kidnap people and take them somewhere deep enough in the swamp where nobody can find them."

"I don't want to believe it's somebody from the

swamp, but I'll admit there are a lot of things that point to that," she replied.

"How many people does that make now who are missing?" Nick asked.

"Six. Six souls that have been lost," she replied. "And that's not counting Colette, who for all intents and purposes is also a lost soul."

"It's wild that this is going on and nobody knows who the bastard is. Now, we'd better change the subject while we finish eating, otherwise we'll both wind up with a bad case of indigestion," he said.

"I agree," she replied.

While they finished their meal, they small-talked about an upcoming celebration Crystal Cove was having. Each year the town had a street fair with booths selling food and people offering handmade items for sale. There was also a carnival with a Ferris wheel and other rides to delight small children and adults alike.

She had always heard it was a great time with neighbors visiting and laughter ringing out in the air. There were gator wrestling contests and baking competitions and a host of other fun things.

"I've never been to the fair before," Heather confessed as they cleared the dishes.

"Really? Then we'll have to plan to go together to this one," he replied. "Why haven't you been before?"

"I figured it wasn't much fun to go alone and all my friends usually had other plans. Then I was nursing my father and taking care of my mother."

Would she really be free to enjoy life after the trial? "It's possible we'll still be in trial when it happens."

"Trust me, trial will be adjourned through the course of the fair. Even Judge Cooke will want to enjoy the festivities. But I have a feeling this is going to be a very short trial, and then we'll celebrate our success by going to the fair," he replied, confidence ringing in his tone.

She looked at him with more than a hint of worry. He grabbed one of her hands. "Take that look off your face right now," he said. "How many times do I need to tell you that I got you?"

"Apparently many times," she replied with a small laugh.

He squeezed her hand and then released it. "By the way, I meant to tell you that you make a really good cuddle buddy."

She laughed once again. "I can say the same thing about you."

His gaze held hers for a long moment. "I wouldn't mind it if you wanted to snuggle with me again tonight."

Her heart lifted and flew with happiness. "I would love to snuggle with you tonight, but only if you wear your aluminum hat for me," she added with an impish grin.

It was his turn to laugh. "Okay, it's a deal."

After breakfast, he disappeared into his office, and Heather sank down on the sofa to watch television. But it was hard to concentrate with the utter happiness that danced in her heart and filled her head.

He had to care about her. Surely a man who wasn't interested wouldn't invite her to his room for the night and wouldn't make plans to see her after the case was over.

He'd told her he planned to be alone for the rest of

his life, but maybe he'd come to that decision because he hadn't found the right woman. And maybe…just maybe she was the right woman for him. At this thought a shiver of delight rushed through her.

She knew with certainty he was the right man for her. She wanted to be with him for the rest of her life. She wanted to spend her days with him and sleep in his arms every night. She longed for a family, and she would give Nick as many babies as he wanted.

Her feelings for Nick had nothing to do with loneliness or gratitude, although she would always be grateful to him for everything he had done and was doing for her. Without him she would probably be dead by now.

At noon Nick came out of his office for some lunch. He made them ham-and-cheese sandwiches, and while they ate, he seemed slightly distant and distracted. He ate quickly and then returned to his office.

Early afternoon passed, and then it was time for her to start cooking dinner. Tonight, she was trying parmesan-encrusted pork chops. Once again, she'd gone to the internet to find a recipe. She was making mashed potatoes, creamed corn and corn muffins as well.

She enjoyed cooking with all the conveniences Nick's kitchen had to offer. It was so different from cooking at her shanty. A wave of homesickness struck her. There was no question that she missed the swamp and her cozy little shanty.

She spoke on the phone fairly regularly to Lucy, but she missed seeing and talking to some of her other friends as well. If she and Nick became a real couple, she would still want to spend time in the swamp. She wasn't sure how it would work between them, but she believed one way or another, things would work out. After all, love conquered all.

It was around five and dinner was ready when Nick came back into the kitchen. "Oh, I was just on my way to tell you dinner is ready."

"The delicious smells called to me," he replied and took a seat at the table. "You've been spoiling me with all these wonderful meals each night."

"I've told you before, I like cooking for you," she replied as she took the pork chops out of the oven. The rest of the meal was already on the table. "At least you're complimentary." She set the chops in the center of the table and then took her seat opposite his.

"I can't help but be complimentary. Your food is always excellent."

"Dig in while it's hot."

They both filled their plates and began to eat. Once again, he was quiet and appeared distracted. Was he worried about the case? Jury selection was right around the corner, followed quickly by the trial. "Is everything all right?" she finally asked.

"Yeah, it's fine. I have a new client coming in tomorrow, and I've been spending my time today getting all the information I can on the case."

"So you'll be in your office in town tomorrow?"

He nodded. "And Bruno will be here with you while I'm gone."

"I'm surprised we didn't see him today. He usually pops in at some time during the day," she said.

"I talked to him on the phone this morning. He had nothing new to report."

"I was hoping he'd find more people who saw that man take me out the back door." She took a drink of her water, swallowing against her disappointment.

"Hopefully, he will find more people before trial. But if we only have the four witnesses, that should be enough to cause reasonable doubt."

There was a confidence in his tone that soothed her fears. She had to believe that he was going to get her off the charges against her. She refused to believe any other scenario. Besides, she believed in Nick.

They finished their meal, and after cleaning up, they moved to the living room, where they watched a movie, and then it was bedtime. He hadn't mentioned any more about her coming into his bedroom to snuggle.

He headed for his bedroom, and she went to hers. She pulled on her nightgown and then washed her face and brushed her teeth. She went back into her bedroom and pulled down the covers, disappointed that she apparently wasn't going to end her day by cuddling with Nick.

She had just slid into the sheets when he called out to her. "Heather...are you coming in here?"

She practically leapt out of the bed. "Yes, yes I am," she replied. She grabbed her purse off the nightstand and hurried toward his bedroom. Since the night the men had broken into her shanty, she'd been carrying the purse everywhere she went. She would never be caught without her daddy's gun again.

She took one step inside his bedroom and dissolved

into a fit of giggles. He sat up in bed, bare chested but wearing a ridiculous aluminum cap on his head. It even had a small bill, making it resemble a ball cap.

She dropped her purse on the floor and fell to the bed as she continued to laugh. "That's hysterical," she said amid giggles.

He looked at her in mock indignation. "Please do not make fun of the item that keeps me safe in case of an alien attack."

"You are such a goof ball," she said.

"Please don't let anyone know. It would ruin my tough-guy reputation," he replied with a wide grin. He swept the hat off his head and placed it on the bed.

"Your secret is safe with me." She picked the hat up and examined it. "When on earth did you have time to make this?"

"I sneaked a roll of foil out of the kitchen after breakfast, and then I spent part of the afternoon fashioning it just for you. I had to do something to hold up my end of the bargain."

"The bargain?"

"You know, the one where I got to snuggle with you, but the payment for the pleasure was letting you see me in that hat."

"Oh, that bargain." She got out of bed and carried the hat to the dresser. "I'm just going to set it right here, so if you feel the presence of aliens, you can easily grab it." She immediately went back to his bed and joined him beneath the sheets.

He turned off the bedside lamp and then pulled her into his arms so he could spoon her. He swept her hair aside and then kissed her on the nape of the neck. "Goodnight, Heather."

"'Night, Nick," she replied. She snuggled into him. This was the way to go to sleep…with laughter in her heart and the man she loved holding her tight. She would gladly exchange the sound of waves lapping against wood and the croak of bullfrogs for the sound of Nick's even breathing next to her.

She awakened the next morning once again alone in the bed. Nick had apparently gotten up again without waking her. The smell of fresh coffee wafted in the air as she left his bedroom and went to her own to get dressed for the day.

There was a lightness in her heart as she went into the kitchen and greeted him. He stood at the stove, cooking sausage patties. "Sausage and waffles," he said.

"Sounds delicious," she replied as she poured herself a cup of coffee. "Is there anything I can do to help?"

"Yeah, you can pour us each a glass of orange juice," he replied. Lordy, but the man looked so hot in his jeans and a white T-shirt. "Other than that, I've got everything under control."

She poured the juice and then sat and watched as he poured thick batter into an awaiting waffle maker. "I'm planning on leaving here around ten this morning. My appointment with the client is at ten thirty, and I should be home by noon."

"So Bruno will be on babysitting duty again," she said.

"He's never had such a beautiful baby to guard," he

said with a grin that flashed his dimples and caused a new warmth to cascade through her.

After breakfast, Nick went back to his bedroom to change his clothes for his meeting in town. When he came back into the living room, he was clad in black slacks, a gray dress shirt and a black suit jacket that she knew hid his holster and gun. He also wore an attractive gray-and-black tie.

"You look all ready for business," she said. He looked ridiculously handsome with a faint aura of danger. She stepped up in front of him and straightened the knot of his tie.

"Thank you," he said.

She smiled up at him. "I can't in good conscience let you go out in public with a crooked tie."

He returned the smile. "And I love that about you."

She stepped back from him, and at that moment there was a knock on the door. It was Bruno, who greeted them both and then sank down on the sofa.

"Bruno, you want coffee or anything to drink?" she asked.

"Nah, I'm good," he replied.

"I should be back around noon," Nick said to his friend.

"Whatever, I'm here for as long as you're gone," Bruno replied.

Minutes later, Nick was gone and Heather sank down on the love seat. "Nick depends on you a lot," she said.

"He's a good man. I depend on him, too."

"He's a wonderful man," Heather replied tremulously. "How did the two of you meet?"

"We met when Nick was in fifth grade and I was in third grade," Bruno said. "At that time, I was a scrawny little kid who got picked on a lot. Meanwhile, everyone liked Nick. He was popular, got good grades and was already a handsome dude. Anyway, one day a couple of older guys were punching around on me, and Nick stepped in. He told them I was one of his best friends, and I was to be left alone."

"Did it work?" Heather asked.

Bruno offered her one of his rare smiles. "Like a charm. We became great friends after that. Then by the time junior high rolled around, I had a big growth spurt and could handle myself without his help."

"It just goes to show again what a wonderful man Nick is," she replied.

Bruno stared at her for a long moment. "You think you're in love with him, don't you?"

Heather's heart quickened. "I don't think so… I know so. I'm in love with him." It felt great to finally admit her feelings out loud. "I am completely in love with him."

Bruno frowned. "Look, Heather, I don't want to see you get hurt, but Nick is fairly unavailable when it comes to love."

Her heart felt like it suddenly stopped beating. "W-what do you mean? He has seemed very available to me."

Bruno shrugged. "You're a beautiful woman living under his roof."

The implication was that Nick was just taking advantage of her. As she thought of all the deep conversations she and Nick had had…all the laughter they had shared, she just couldn't believe it. She knew Nick cared about her on a much deeper level. In fact, she believed he was falling in love with her, too.

"It's more than that between us," she finally said in protest.

Bruno leaned forward. "Nick will never again trust a woman enough to get married, especially if that woman is a client of his."

"But, why?" she asked and stared at the bald man inquisitively.

"Has he told you about Delia?" He leaned back again. She frowned. "Delia? Who is Delia?"

"So he hasn't told you about Delia Hunter." She shook her head. "She was a client of his several years ago."

"What about her?" she asked in confusion. What would an old client have to do with the here and now and what was on going on between her and Nick?

"Ask Nick. It's not my story to tell," Bruno replied. "I'm just telling you this because I don't want to see you get hurt, and I don't want my friend to get hurt."

"I would never…could never hurt Nick. I owe him so much for everything he has done for me."

"Are you sure your love for him isn't just a huge amount of gratitude?" He looked at her long and hard. "I would think in these circumstances it would be easy to mistake the two."

"Trust me, what I feel for him isn't simple gratitude," she replied. "It's so much more than that."

"See how you feel about things once the trial is over," he replied. "And now I'm done talking about it," he replied. "I already said too much as it is. Why don't you turn on one of your shows to watch until Nick gets back here."

She turned on the television, but there was no way she could concentrate on a show when so many thoughts were racing in her head.

She knew her heart where Nick was concerned. She was definitely grateful to him, but aside from her gratitude, her love for him continued to grow each and every day.

Was Nick just using her because she was pretty and available? Because she was swamp and therefore easy to use and then eventually discard when this was all over?

She found that hard to believe. Nick just wasn't that kind of man. He was an honorable man who would never use a woman like that. Or did he have her completely fooled? Still, there was one question that whirled around and around in her head. Who in the heck was Delia Hunter?

NICK WAS UNIMPRESSED with his new client. He'd already overheard Brett Mayfield talking crap about Heather and people from the swamp when he'd been in the café. Now the man needed representation due to a bar fight that saw him arrested.

The fight had occurred in a seedy bar located on the west side of town. Nick had never even been in Ralph's Brewery, where the parking lot was usually filled with big motorcycles and pickup trucks.

Once again Tommy Radcliffe had thrown the book at the man, charging him with assault and battery for beating down a man. From what Nick had learned, it was a typical bar fight with fists thrown by a lot of boozed-up hotheads.

"Radcliffe is just picking on me," the big man whined. "I was only defending myself. That crazy Dax Patrick came at me. I don't even know what he's doing in Crystal Cove. He's a creep and an outsider and doesn't belong here."

"I'll see what I can do to get the charges changed to a misdemeanor," Nick replied.

"I got money. I can afford to pay a big fine. That's the only reason why Radcliffe charged me and not that creep Dax. Besides, I wasn't the only one throwing fists that night. There were a lot of men throwing down."

"Let's get this all taken care of." Nick had the man sign the appropriate paperwork. "From the notes I got from your arraignment, the trial is set for a month away. However, I'm hoping we won't have to go to trial. I'll be in touch with you in the next couple of days," he said as Brett stood to leave.

"And I'll be waiting to hear from you," Brett replied and then left his office. Brett was a big meathead, hot-headed and ready to punch people, especially when booze was added to the mix. Still, Nick was fairly sure it would never get to trial. He would call Tommy in the next day or two and see what they could work out. He imagined Tommy would be okay with a large fine paid by Brett.

Sharon knocked on his door and then came into his office. She had been keeping the office open for new walk-in clients while Nick had been working from home.

"Heard you had a date the other night," he said to her and gestured to the chair in front of his desk.

"I did." She sat. "Do you mind? About me and Bruno?"

"Why on earth would I mind?" he asked.

"I wasn't sure if you were okay with us fraternizing with each other outside of work hours," she replied.

"Even big-muscled bald guys need love," he replied with a grin.

She laughed. "It's not that deep yet. It was just one date, although he did invite me to get ice cream with him tomorrow night. Uh…did he say anything to you about me?"

"No, he's playing it close to his chest. You know how he is, Sharon. He doesn't talk much and especially not about his feelings. But I would say the fact that he asked you out again means he enjoyed your company."

Her cheeks pinkened. "I really enjoyed his company, too."

"Speaking of feelings, how are things going between you and Heather? It must be difficult sharing your space after living alone for so long."

"She makes it incredibly easy. She's the perfect houseguest, and we get along great." Too great, he thought to himself.

"Are you ready for trial?" Sharon asked.

"Yeah, in fact I'm going to be sending you a lot of things in the next week or so to prepare for the big day."

"I stand ready to serve," she replied.

"That's good because you know I depend on you," Nick replied. "And now I'd better get out of here. I've got Bruno with Heather, and the two of them still aren't very comfortable with each other."

He stood, along with Sharon. She returned to her desk in the front, and he left the office. As he drove home, his thoughts were filled with Heather.

He had been so determined to distance himself from her, but he'd failed at that miserably. When he smelled her perfume all day long and enjoyed every minute he spent in her company, it was damned difficult to deprive himself of her.

Besides, it wouldn't be long now before her trial was over. At that time, she would return to her life and her shanty in the swamp, and their time together would be over.

His chest tightened as he thought about no longer having her in his world. He couldn't be in love with her because he refused to believe in love again. He would never trust in a woman's love again, especially a client's love. Fool me once, shame on you. Fool me twice, shame on me.

He just wanted to enjoy her now, and then he would let her go so she could find a man who was emotionally available to her…somebody who wasn't in charge of her future…a man she wasn't grateful to.

As always when he drove down his street, he looked for potential danger. This quiet that was going on right now from the killer felt loaded. The closer they got to trial, the more dangerous he would be. If he was afraid of what Heather might testify to, then he was going to make a move to silence her permanently and soon. Somehow, they all had to be ready for it.

Unfortunately, Etienne and his men hadn't found any clues or leads to follow about the men who had tried to break into Heather's shanty. So, nothing had come from that investigation.

He saw no strange cars and nobody to give him pause on the street, and so he pulled into his garage, parked and closed the door behind him.

He had to keep her safe, and he had to get her off the charges. At this moment in time, he wasn't sure what was going to be more difficult.

He got out of his car and went inside to find Bruno and Heather in the living room. They were watching a show on television, and the moment she saw him she reached for the remote and hit the pause button.

"That was quick. How did your meeting go?" she asked.

"It went fine." He pulled on the knot of his tie and unfastened it. "How are things here?" He looked at Bruno and then back at her. He sensed a weird kind of tension in the air.

"Things are fine, except she's got me watching some reality show," Bruno replied and immediately stood. "Now that you're home, I'll just get out of here. I'm assuming we're doing surveillance duty tonight."

"That's the plan," Nick said as he walked his friend to the door.

"Okay, then I'll see you tonight." With that, Bruno left.

Nick walked back into the living room. "I'm going to go change into more comfortable clothes, and then I'll be right back," he said.

"Okay," she replied.

He changed into jeans and a gray T-shirt and then returned to the living room. He sank down on the sofa next to her and smiled. "Anything exciting happen while I was gone?"

"No, nothing, but in just a few minutes I need to get into the kitchen and put dinner in to cook."

"And what culinary delight are you making for dinner tonight?"

"Smothered steak and potatoes, corn and salad."

"Hmm, sounds delicious. You know if you ever tire of making the evening meals, I can take over."

"No, I really enjoy cooking for you. However, I must say that your freezer is getting fairly empty, and tonight will be the last of the fresh lettuce."

"I'll make a grocery order tonight and have it delivered tomorrow."

She looked at him in surprise. "The store will do that? Bring groceries to your doorstep?"

He laughed. "They will if you pay extra for the pleasure of home delivery."

"I wonder how much it would cost to get groceries delivered to me in the swamp."

"Probably a lot," he replied.

"You're probably right," she said. "If you order some fish, I can fix my awesome fried fish for dinner one night."

"Awesome fried fish, now that sounds like a plan," he replied.

She smiled. "On that note, I think I'll get busy in the kitchen."

"It's awfully early for you to start cooking dinner," he observed.

"I know. I'm mostly just doing some preparation work, and then I'll actually cook it all later this afternoon," she explained.

"And I'm going to go do a little work in my office," he replied. "So I'll just see you later."

"Later," she echoed. They both got off the sofa. She headed for the kitchen, and he went down the hall to his office. For the next two hours, he got most of the information he would need to defend Brett Mayfield and then worked on his opening statement for Heather's trial.

He'd hoped that Heather's trial would never happen. He'd hoped the charges would be dropped, but it looked like nothing was going to stop it now.

The opening statement was one of the most important things in a trial. It told the jurors what his case was and how they were going to prove Heather's innocence. He'd been writing and rewriting it for the past week, needing to make sure he got it all exactly right.

He'd had the subpoenas served on the four witnesses who saw Heather with the man going out the back door. He would like to have an interview with each of them before trial, but he'd called them all, and they told him they didn't want to talk unless they had to and that would be under oath.

He was starting to feel as if all the cards were stacked against them. Etienne was too busy with the other big crime going on, Tommy was being a stubborn jerk and witnesses didn't want to talk. At this point, what else could go wrong?

By the time Heather called him for dinner, his stomach was growling with hunger and he was ready to knock off for the day. He went into the kitchen, where she was placing dinner on the table.

"Hmm, smells good," he said as he sank down in his chair at the table.

"This is something I cook occasionally for myself at home since it's a skillet dish," she replied.

She joined him at the table, and they began to eat. The steak was incredibly tender, as were the chunks of potatoes and mushrooms. It was all covered with a thick, flavorful gravy.

"This is really good," he said.

"Thanks," she replied succinctly.

Something was off. She was unnaturally quiet through the meal. Even though he tried to make small talk with her as they ate, she appeared distracted and distant. Her energy felt low, and even when he tried to get her to laugh by saying something silly, her response was lackluster.

With everything that was going on in her life, she certainly deserved to have an off day. But it bothered him. He wanted to know what was going on in her pretty head. He wanted to somehow make it better.

He waited to say anything to her until dinner was done and the dishes were cleared. They moved into the living room and decided on a movie, but before he hit Play, he leaned over and took her hand in his.

"Heather, is anything wrong? You were unusually quiet through dinner. You seem preoccupied. Are you worried about anything? Is there something I can do to help?"

Her eyes were unusually dark as she held his gaze for a long moment. "No, I've just been thinking about what's going to happen. Even if you win my case, I'm trying to figure out exactly how I'll pick up the pieces of my life. Will there be some people in town who believe I'm guilty of something even after my trial? Will people maybe think I conspired with that guy to kill Wesley? Will anyone ever shop at my store again?"

"Whoa," Nick said and squeezed her hand tightly. She was obviously getting more and more upset with every sentence she spoke. "Honey, when this is all over and you've been found innocent, there's no question in my mind that you will easily be able to pick up the pieces. You are such a strong woman, Heather. I know you'll be fine, and people will return to getting their fresh herbs from you. Something else will come along for people to talk about. Please believe me, you're going to be just fine." He gave her hand another tight squeeze, and then he released it.

She let go of a tremulous sigh and then held his gaze for another long moment. "Who is Delia?"

Shock sat him upright at the name from his past. As Heather held his gaze expectantly, he realized he was going to have to tell her about his painful love story.

Chapter Twelve

Heather saw the utter surprise that overtook his features, and then he released what sounded like a weary sigh. "I guess my partner has a big mouth," he said.

"He just mentioned her in passing and I was naturally curious," she replied. She was more than curious. She needed to know about the woman who, according to Bruno, kept Nick from ever wanting to commit to anyone else.

He broke his gaze from hers and instead stared off into the space just above her right shoulder. "She was a client of mine, and she'd been charged with breaking and entering into an apartment and badly beating the woman inside. Apparently the two had heated words with one another over a fender bender in the grocery store parking lot. She insisted she was innocent of the charges against her, and I immediately believed her. She was a beautiful woman, and in the two months before her trial started, we grew very close."

"You were in love with her," Heather said softly.

He looked back at her and slowly nodded his head. "Yeah, I was. I thought she was the one…the woman I'd been waiting for. I wanted to marry her and build a future with her. I wanted her to have my babies. She seemed to want the same things, and I was sure when her trial was over, we were going to have a very happy life together forever."

He gazed away from her again and cleared his throat. "Anyway, that didn't happen. I won at her trial, and she was cleared of all charges against her. It was then she confessed to me that she'd only acted like she was in love with me so that I would work my hardest to get her off. She told me she was grateful for all my hard work, and then the next day she left town with another man. And that's the story of Delia."

"She broke your heart badly," Heather said softly.

Once again, he looked at her. "Yeah, she did," he agreed.

She felt his pain. It emanated off him in waves and dulled the blue of his eyes. She hurt for him, and now she understood what Bruno had said…about Nick being emotionally unavailable to another woman, especially one who was his client.

"Nick, I'm so sorry that happened to you, but not all women are like her," she said.

He released a small, dry laugh. "Logically I know that, but the heart remains wary."

"I could never pretend to love a man no matter how high the stakes were for me," she said fervently. She leaned toward him, fighting her impulse to touch him in some way.

"It was an evil thing for her to do, but, Nick, you shouldn't close your heart off to giving and receiving love because of her."

She wanted to say so much more to him. She wanted to bare her heart and soul to him. She desperately wanted to tell him that she was deeply in love with him. But this wasn't the time for that…not now when his heart was so heavy with memories of a past betrayal.

"I'm so sorry that happened to you, Nick. You didn't deserve that," she finally said.

He smiled at her and reached out to touch a strand of her hair. "You're a very nice woman, Heather."

She returned his smile. "I'm glad you realize that."

He dropped his hand and cleared his throat once again. "Ready to watch another show?" he asked. "We have plenty of time before Bruno gets here for surveillance."

"Sure," she replied, although she could think of many other ways to pass the time before surveillance. She'd like to stroke the side of his face until the darkness in his eyes lifted. She wanted to take him in her arms and hold him tight. She wanted to kiss him with enough passion that he would forget Delia's name.

Instead, she focused on the crime drama he'd put on for them to watch. She'd been watching it for several minutes when a remembered scent filled her head.

"Spearmint," she suddenly said. "The man who carried me out into the alley smelled of beer and spearmint. I just remembered that."

He paused the show and turned to her. "And Etienne found spearmint gum wrappers in a parking space across the street from your shop on the day we were shot at."

"So it was likely the same man. Oh, I wish I could remember more about that night," she said miserably.

"I know you're doing the best you can. Heather, even if you don't remember another single thing, we might have enough evidence to beat the charges. We have four witnesses who corroborate the fact that a man was in that alley with you and Wesley, and that's a real game changer."

"I just want the man who killed Wesley, the man who has tried to kill me, behind bars," she replied. "He needs to go away for the rest of his life for what he's done."

"I definitely agree with you, and once the charges against you are dropped then Etienne will have no other choice but to reopen the case. He'll find this guy, and justice will be served."

"I hope so," she replied fervently.

He put the show back on, but her thoughts whirled around and around in her head, making it impossible for her to focus on the drama taking place on screen.

Her thoughts continued to be tangled in her head as they parked at the drug house for another night of surveillance. Bruno and Nick talked softly about past cases they'd worked on, and she tried to sort out all the information she'd gained about Nick.

That Delia woman had apparently done a real number on his head. She understood now why Nick would be so wary about getting involved with another client again.

And yet they were involved. He could pretend he didn't care about her, but Heather knew better. Despite what Delia had done to him, Heather believed he had healed and his heart was once again open.

Was he afraid she was another Delia just pretending

to care about him, and once he won her case, she would dip out of his life forever? All she could do was continue to show him her love and hope it broke through any doubts he might have about her.

She wouldn't speak the actual words to him until her case was over. Then he would know for sure that her case had nothing to do with her love for him.

These thoughts were interrupted as a car pulled up to the house. She leaned forward with anticipation and then slumped back in the seat as a young woman got out of the car.

Heather popped a little cinnamon bear in her mouth and chewed the sweet. This whole thing felt like such a waste of time. They really had no clue if the man they sought was part of the drug world. They had no idea if he would eventually come to this run-down house. They could be spinning their wheels all for nothing with these surveillances.

They were only guessing that he fought with Wesley that night over drugs and money owed. The two men might have been fighting over something else altogether. So far, Bruno had found nobody who was willing to talk to him about Wesley's drug abuse.

"They're all afraid of self-incrimination," Bruno had said. "Apparently the drug problem among the upper crust here in Crystal Coves is a dirty little secret."

It was now close to midnight, and the moon shone down a beautiful illumination. Suddenly a wave of homesickness struck her and tightened her chest.

She missed seeing the moonlight dance on the dark swamp waters at night. She also missed seeing the early morning sun painting everything with a golden gild. There was no place as beautiful as where she lived, with its vivid green colors and the lacy Spanish moss. When this was all over, she'd dance on her porch and breathe in the scents of home. And if things didn't work out with Nick, she'd mourn deep and long over the fact that he was gone from her life.

The door to the house flew open, and two men stepped out on the rickety front porch. They were both big men, and they were armed.

Oh God, she thought. If they decided to do a street patrol now, it wasn't going to end as well as it had last time, unless Nick decided to plant a big kiss on Bruno.

"Something is about to happen," Bruno said, his voice low and taut.

"Yeah, but what?" Nick replied, his voice also filled with tension.

Heather leaned forward and started chewing her nail as nervous tension filled her. The men remained standing outside, obviously on some kind of guard duty. But what or who were they guarding?

About fifteen minutes later, a car pulled up out front. Heather watched the man who got out of the car. "It's him," she exclaimed with excitement. She leaned forward and gripped Nick's shoulder. "That's the man who carried me out of the back door that night."

"Are you sure?" Nick asked.

"I'm positive," she replied and squeezed his shoulder.

Bruno raised the fancy camera he always had with him on surveillance nights and began to take photos until the man disappeared into the house.

"I mostly got pictures of his back. I'm hoping to get better ones when he comes back out of the house," Bruno said.

"Then we'll have the pictures to take to Etienne," Nick replied with his own excitement.

The man was only in the house for about ten minutes and then he exited. Once again, Bruno's camera clicked and whirred, only stopping when the man disappeared into the car. The two guards immediately went back into the house.

"I'll see if I can get a picture of the license plate," Bruno said, and he took more photos as the man drove off.

"Finally, some success," Nick said.

"About time," Bruno replied.

Excitement winged through Heather's blood as well. The time spent here had been a success, and soon the man would be identified.

"Now we can get out of here. We'll go to my place and have a celebratory drink." Nick started the car.

"Sounds like a plan to me," Bruno said.

Heather really hoped Bruno had gotten some good photos and they could find out the man's name. She was certain he had killed Wesley in that alley and had tried to kill her. Hopefully Etienne could get him into custody, not only to once and for all prove her innocence, but also to make sure the man would never try to kill her again. Or anyone else.

They got back to the house, and Nick made drinks for them all. Heather sipped on the whiskey and soda while Nick and Bruno looked at the pictures in the camera.

"Boom," Nick said at one point. "That's a perfect one for us to get him identified." He moved away from Bruno. "Can you have these all printed out by morning?"

"I can. How about I plan on meeting you here around nine in the morning with the prints?"

"That would be great, and you can stick around here while I take them to Etienne?" Nick asked.

"Definitely." Bruno downed the last of his drink and stood. "I'd better get out of here now so I can have things ready in the morning."

Nick set his drink down and also stood. "I'll walk you out."

A moment later, Nick returned to the room and smiled at her. It was one of his full-dimpled smiles that rushed a sweet heat through her. "What a great night," he said.

"Definitely," she replied.

"There's only one thing that would make it better."

"And what's that?" she asked.

"It will make it a perfect night if I can fall asleep next to you."

She smiled at him. "I totally feel the same way."

"Then let's go to bed." He held out a hand to her and pulled her up and off the sofa. She grabbed her purse, and then together they headed down the hallway.

Minutes later, Nick was spooned around her, sound asleep. Surely, she was making ways into his heart. Bruno was wrong about his friend. She believed Nick was open and ready to love again, and she truly believed Nick loved her.

To think this was all temporary and just a dream that would end hurt her heart. They were about to catch the killer, and that would exonerate her, but in the end, would she be left all alone and brokenhearted?

"THIS IS A photo of the man who was in that alley with Heather and Wesley," Nick said the next morning as he handed Etienne one of the photos they had taken the night before.

Etienne took the photo from him. He frowned and looked back at Nick. "And how do you know this?"

"Heather positively identified him as the man who took her out in the alley. He was coming out of the drug house on 22nd Street. We've had the house under surveillance for some time now, figuring he might show up there," Nick explained.

"Dammit, Nick, don't you know how dangerous that might be?" Etienne gave him a dark, disapproving look.

"I had Bruno with me," Nick replied.

"I don't care. It was still damned dangerous," Etienne said.

"But successful," Nick said with a grin.

Etienne released a deep sigh and then looked at the picture. "I don't recognize him. I don't suppose Heather remembered his name?"

"I don't think she ever knew his name. According to her, she didn't speak to him before all this happened. And I'll bet you a dollar when you find him you'll discover he chews spearmint gum."

"I'll give copies of this to my officers and see if we can get a name on this guy."

"Can you also show it to the four people I've sub-poenaed? They won't talk to me right now, but I'd like to get confirmation from them that this is the man they saw helping Heather out the back door at the Voodoo Lounge that night."

"I can do that," the lawman agreed.

"Anything moving on the Soul Stealer case?"

Once again Etienne frowned. "Nothing. I swear this man moves like a ghost through the night. He man-ages to take control of people without a sound and then whisk them away without leaving a single clue behind."

"And still no movement from Colette."

Etienne shook his head. "Nothing. I've been spend-ing my nights in her hospital room, holding her hand and talking to her. I'm hoping the human touch and the sound of my voice will somehow assure her and call her back to consciousness." He released a dry, slightly embarrassed laugh. "I know it sounds stupid."

"Not at all," Nick replied. "And for everyone's sake, I hope it works." Nick couldn't stand the idea of Heather returning to the swamp with this madman at work. He couldn't stand the idea of anything bad ever happen-ing to her again.

"I'll just get out of here and let you get back to work. You'll call me if any of your officers find out the iden-tity of this guy?"

"Definitely, and if your witnesses all identify him as the man who took Heather out into the alley, then I'll encourage Tommy to drop the charges against her, and I'll reopen the case."

"That's definitely music to my ears," Nick replied and stood. "Then I'll talk to you later."

"Later," Etienne agreed.

Nick walked out into the late morning sunshine feeling more optimistic about the fact that Heather's case was probably never going to trial. While he was confident that, in the end, he would have been successful in getting her off, having the charges dropped was now in the best interest of justice.

He fully expected to get a phone call from Tommy in the next day or two telling him the charges against Heather had been dropped and the case had been reopened.

As he was walking to his car, he passed a jewelry shop and had a sudden desire to go in and buy something for Heather in celebration. He entered the shop and was greeted by Mollie LeBlanc.

"Hey, Mollie, it's nice to see you again," he said, remembering her from the night he had met all of Heather's friends. "But I thought you clerked at the grocery store."

"I did, but I quit to come here and work. I figured the odds of meeting the wealthy man who is going to marry me and get me out of the swamp were better selling jewelry here instead of ringing up fish at the grocery store."

He laughed. "Has it worked yet? Have you met that special wealthy guy?"

"Nah, but a girl can always hope. Now, what can I get for you today?"

"I wanted to look at your gold necklaces," he said. Heather didn't wear a necklace presumably because she didn't have one. He could only imagine the beauty of the gold against her beautiful olive skin.

"Is this for you?" Mollie asked.

"No, actually it's for Heather," he replied.

Mollie's eyes widened. "Oh, that's so nice. She will love it." She cast him a sly smile. "Is there a special reason for the gift?"

"We've become good friends, and she's been through so much, so I just wanted to do something nice for her," he replied, hoping no gossip would follow this purchase.

Mollie led him to a glass display case that held an array of gold necklaces. There were different sizes and lengths to consider. After some thought, he finally settled on one, and once Mollie had placed it into a gift box, he left the store.

What are you doing, man? He asked himself as he drove home. What in the hell was he doing with Heather? He was in love with her. The realization suddenly hit him like a ton of bricks over his head.

Oh God, he'd tried to keep his heart away from her. He'd tried to shield himself from the very emotions he now realized he harbored deep in his heart for her.

But he had no willpower where she was concerned. He thought it was all about desiring her physically. But he now realized he wanted to spend each and every minute during the day with her and to wrap her in his arms every night. He wanted to laugh with her for the rest of his life. He'd been a stupid fool.

Yes, he was in love with her, but he would never trust that she loved him back. Oh, she might believe herself to be in love with him, but he would never believe that her love hadn't grown out of deep gratitude and would disappear once she was finally safe and free.

This was the beginning of the end. Their time together was growing to a close. Within days, she could potentially go back to the swamp. She didn't know it, but she would take his heart with her.

He would never let anyone know the depths of his love for her and how badly he would mourn when she was gone. He would hide his feelings deep inside. He had known better than to mix business with pleasure, but he'd allowed himself to blur those lines, and now he would pay the consequences for that.

The necklace he'd bought her would be a goodbye gift, and maybe when she wore it, she would occasionally think of the lawyer who had helped her out when she had no other place to go…the man who had believed in her innocence despite all evidence to the contrary.

He pulled into his garage and pocketed the gift box. When he walked in, Bruno and Heather were in their usual places in the living room.

"How did it go?" Bruno asked him.

"Better than expected," he replied and sank down on the sofa next to the big man. "Etienne is going to have all his officers flashing the photo around town to see if they can get the man's name. He's also going to encourage Tommy to drop the charges against you," he said to Heather.

"That would be amazing," she replied, a happy light dancing in her eyes.

"Yeah, that means within the next few days you

could be back in your shanty and resuming your life again," he said.

"That would be nice," she replied, although Nick could have sworn the sparkle in her eyes dimmed a bit. Still, it could have just been a trick of the light.

"It will be nice for us all to get back to our own normal lives," Bruno said.

"Amen to that," Nick added.

Moments later Bruno had gone, and Nick and Heather were alone again. "While I was out, I bought you a little present," he said.

Her eyes widened. "A present for me? Why?"

"Because I wanted to and as a celebration of sorts," he replied. He got up and pulled the gift box out of his pocket. He took the lid off and crouched down beside her so she could see what was inside.

"Oh, Nick…it's beautiful, but I can't accept that from you," she protested.

"And why not?" he asked.

"Because it's obviously expensive, and I already owe you so much," she said.

"So you would take away my pleasure in giving you a gift? Come on, Heather. Don't take away my joy. Besides, it will look beautiful on you, and I wanted you to have something from me when this is all over." He unfastened it and took it out of the box. "Now, move your hair aside so I can put it on you."

She swept her long mane aside, and he fastened the necklace on her. "There," he said as he stepped back from her. "Just as I figured, it looks beautiful on your skin."

She touched the necklace with her fingertips. "Thank you, Nick. I'll wear it always."

He simply couldn't help himself. He pulled her up and off the sofa and into his arms. She immediately molded herself to him and wrapped her arms around his neck.

"I can't believe it's almost over," she said softly. "It's been a nightmare, and yet it's also been a wonderful dream all at the same time."

"I agree, but even wonderful dreams have to come to an end," he said and released his hold on her. He had to stop touching her…stop wanting her before he got in any deeper. It was just a matter of days before she went back to her life in the swamp, and their time together would end.

It was best that way. She deserved a man who would love her without restraint, and he told himself it simply wasn't going to be him. Soon after, he went into his office and she went into the kitchen. He heard the ding of a message on his phone, and when he opened it, it was an alert to let him know his groceries were arriving.

He had requested contactless delivery, and ten minutes later he watched out the peep hole of the front door as a young man lined up the plastic bags on his porch. He recognized the man as someone who had delivered to him before.

When he was gone, Nick cautiously opened his door, his gun at the ready. Until Etienne had the bad guy in custody, there was still the possibility of danger. This would be a perfect opportunity for somebody to rush his door.

He gazed all around the area, and seeing nobody anywhere around, he quickly pulled the bags inside and then closed and relocked the door. He carried the bags into the kitchen. "Special delivery," he said as he placed the groceries on the kitchen table.

He'd decided to keep things as light and simple as possible after the emotional morning. He'd let her know in so many ways now that an ongoing relationship between the two of them wasn't going to happen, that this magic they had going on between them was, indeed, coming to an end.

He'd hoped to get a phone call from Etienne telling him the man in the photo had been identified, but by dinner time that still hadn't happened.

She'd fixed another delicious meal. The roast was tender and served with rich brown gravy. Mashed potatoes and a vegetable medley rounded out the supper.

"I'm definitely going to miss your cooking," he said.

"I'm sure you'll be just fine cooking for yourself," she replied.

They fell silent for a few minutes as they focused on eating. He couldn't get a read on her mood. She was quiet and appeared pensive. He had a feeling he'd hurt her with all his talk of her going home.

The very last thing he'd ever wanted to do was hurt Heather. But he'd warned her that he wasn't in the market for a wife. He'd told her early on that he wasn't promising her anything.

He couldn't help it that their relationship had deepened and grown. She would eventually realize he did her a favor by making her go. She would eventually realize that any feelings she had toward him were tangled up with feelings of gratitude.

It was possible she was ready to go home, back to the swamp that she loved. It was possible she was more than ready to leave here....leave him. After all, she'd never told him she was in love with him. Maybe he was just a conceited jerk for believing she might be.

"Are you okay?" he finally asked.

She looked up at him and smiled. "I'm fine. I'm just a bit tired."

"Just think, there's no more need for middle-of-the-night surveillance, so tonight we can go to bed at a reasonable hour and get a good night's sleep."

"That sounds absolutely wonderful," she replied.

They finished eating and then cleaned up the kitchen and went into the living room. "I thought that maybe tonight instead of watching a movie, maybe I could teach you a little chess," he suggested.

"That sounds like fun. But I'm only interested on one condition. You teach me chess for an hour, and I teach you how to dance for an hour." She cast him an impish smile. Oh, he loved it when her eyes sparkled with humor and she looked so happy.

He laughed. "Okay, it's a deal." He got his chessboard out of a cabinet that was set against one wall.

She watched as he set it all up on the coffee table. "My father used to play chess with a couple of his buddies when I was younger," she said. "I always thought it looked intriguing, but he never taught me to play."

"I find it intriguing," he replied. "It's definitely a game of strategy."

"Then that explains why you like it," she replied. "As a lawyer, I'm sure you're all about strategy."

He laughed. "Maybe a little bit."

He then began to explain to her how the game was played and how the different pieces moved. Just as he suspected, she was a quick study. After a half an hour of explaining how each piece moved, they began to play their first game.

He easily beat her. The second game, she made several smart adjustments to her play, but once again he beat her. But by the third game, he had to work hard to win against her. They quit playing after he won the fourth game.

"You wait and see, I'll beat you when we play again," she replied boastfully as they cleared off the game from the coffee table. "Okay, I now know how to play chess, so it's time to see how you dance. Can you put on some music for us to dance to?" Her eyes shone merrily.

He got up and turned his stereo on. It immediately piped an oldies song through the house. She remained sitting on the sofa, her eyes bright. "Why don't you show me how you would dance to this, and then I'll know how much work I have ahead of me."

"Okay." He intentionally moved as awkwardly as he could, flailing his arms and legs around and setting her into a bout of giggles. "Stop," she cried between laughs. "Please stop…you're doing that on purpose."

"Then get up and show me how it's done," he replied.

She rose to her feet and took his hands in hers. "Just sway and get a feel for the music," she instructed.

He swayed with her, and then she showed him several steps and they began to dance. He was never going to get a job as a professional dancer, but after several fast songs he felt good about the fact that at least he wouldn't make a total fool out of himself on the dance floor in the future.

Then a slow song came on, and he pulled her into his arms. "This, I know how to do," he said softly. She fit so perfectly against him, and the sweet scent of her hair...of her...dizzied all his senses.

When she looked up at him, he took her lips in a tender kiss, and then he released her. "I think that's enough dancing for one night. I don't know about you, but I'm ready for bed."

"Me, too," she agreed. "Am I sleeping in your room?"

He should tell her no, start the distancing that needed to happen right now, but she definitely was his biggest weakness. Even if they didn't make love, he loved falling asleep with her in his arms.

"I would love for you to sleep in my bed," he replied, helpless against his own desire for her.

It would soon be all over, but for tonight he would sleep with her in his arms and cherish the moments he had left with her.

Chapter Thirteen

Heather snuggled into Nick's arms. He had already fallen asleep, but despite her tiredness, she was finding sleep elusive. This had been the most difficult day she'd spent with Nick. He'd broken her heart in a million different little ways, and she'd had to fight hard to hide it.

He'd made it very obvious that he had no intention of continuing to pursue a relationship with her once this was all over. Somehow, she had hoped that he would profess his undying love for her, and they would live happily-ever-after. But that hadn't happened, and she knew now it wasn't going to happen.

She would return to her shanty all alone, and it was going to take her a very long time to get over loving him. And it was only when she was back in her familiar shanty that she would allow her tears of heartbreak to fall.

She would cry long and hard for the man she loved who didn't love her back. Yet, until today, she'd been so sure that he loved her. Oh, he hadn't said the words out loud, but it had been in the way she caught him gazing at her when he thought she wasn't looking. She'd felt his love every time he touched her in the simplest way. The necklace had felt like a gift of love from him. But apparently, it had been a present of goodbye. She'd been wrong to believe that he loved her as he'd made it clear throughout the entire day that he was letting her go.

She must have drifted off to sleep because a jarring siren noise awakened her. Nick was immediately up and out of the bed. "Somebody is breaking in," he yelled as he grabbed his gun from the nightstand. "Stay in here and call Etienne."

Her heart banged against her ribs in an accelerated rhythm as the siren continued to blare through the house. "No, Nick," she yelled as he peeked outside the door.

Even the siren couldn't hide the sound of a gunshot. Oh God, they were not only in the house, but they were also firing bullets in the direction of their bedroom.

She didn't have to be a rocket scientist to guess who it was, and right now she and Nick were trapped in the bedroom at the end of the long hallway. Eventually it would be easy for a man or men to creep down the hallway and get into this room where she and Nick would be sitting ducks.

She jumped off the bed and retrieved her phone from her purse. She quickly made the call to the police station and then pulled out her daddy's gun.

The house was dark except for the moonlight that drifted through the windows. Nick slid out into the hallway, and the sound of gunfire went off. One…two… three shots. Oh God, had Nick been hit?

On trembling legs, she ran to the doorway and peeked out. "Nick," she screamed as she saw no sign of him. Was he lying on the floor in the darkness? Bleeding to death or already dead from a gunshot wound? "Nick," she cried once again in desperation.

"Stay there, Heather," he yelled back. He'd apparently made it into the bathroom next to the bedroom. Another shot rang out, the bullet splintering the doorjamb next to where she stood. She screamed and stepped back into the bedroom.

Her fear tightened her chest, making it impossible for her to draw a deep breath. She panted, her abject terror, not just for herself, but also for Nick, ripping through her very soul.

The siren screeching overhead only added to the melee. What was Nick doing? Why had he left the bedroom? Was he trying to be some sort of hero? Facing the bad guys before they could get to her? He could be killed attempting to save her. The very last thing she wanted was a dead hero...a dead Nick. The very thought horrified her.

She gripped her gun more firmly in her hand. More gunfire sounded, and once again she peeked out of the room and down the hallway. The air there was smoky and smelled acrid from the gunpowder.

"Nick," she screamed once again, needing to assure herself he was still alive.

"I'm here," he yelled back from the same position.

As Heather watched the hallway, she saw a dark figure in the distance. She raised her gun and fired at him. She wasn't going to just sit on the bed and allow Nick to be killed by a thug who wanted her dead. She would do whatever she could to help Nick.

She stepped back into the room as answering gun-shots fired back. "Heather…cover me," Nick yelled just loud enough for her to hear. Once again, she leaned out of the room and began to shoot as Nick quickly left the bathroom and raced across the hall into his office.

She suspected his plan. He wanted to back them up farther away from the bedroom where she was located. She now believed there were two shooters. Their guns sounded slightly different. She knew with certainty one of them was the man who had killed Wesley.

Her nerves had calmed a bit beneath a steely resolve to make sure she and Nick walked out of this madness alive. She breathed slowly, in through her nose and out through her mouth. She wanted to weep and scream, but she could fall apart later. Right now, Nick needed her to keep her head about her.

She looked out again and saw a figure rushing toward Nick's office. She closed her eyes and fired four shots, one right after the other. When she opened her eyes again, she saw a dark figure on the floor. Smoke swirled in the dark air, making it impossible for her to discern if it was Nick.

Oh God, was it Nick? Had she inadvertently shot him? Her heart seemed to stop beating. Had she accidentally killed the man she loved?

Then the man began to scream in pain. A shudder of deep relief rushed through her. Thank God it wasn't Nick. She lowered her gun, her knees weak with fear and the unknown.

The screaming siren overhead suddenly stopped, and the house was silent except for the man she had shot.

"Get me an ambulance," he cried. "Dammit, I'm hurt and I need some help here."

"Don't trust him, Nick," she yelled. "It could be a ruse." At that moment, the sound of other sirens pierced the night. It was the sound of approaching police.

Heather sank to the floor as a rush of deep relief flowed through her veins, although she still tightly gripped her gun and watched the doorway.

Within minutes, all the lights in the house were turned on, and police filled the place. She got back up to her feet, although her legs were still shaky.

It wasn't until Etienne disarmed the man in the hallway, with the bright lights gleaming overhead, that she finally saw who she had shot. It was him...the man who had killed Wesley.

She raised her gun. Now he was the sitting duck, and there was nothing more she would like to do than put a bullet in his evil heart. Her hand began to shake, and she finally lowered the gun. She couldn't shoot him. She wasn't like him.

She tossed the gun on Nick's bed and then left the room.

Nick met her in the hallway, and she collapsed in his arms, crying the tears she'd held in during the entire ordeal. He held her tight against him, stroking her back. "It's okay, Heather. We're safe now. It's finally over."

He led her to Etienne, who stood over the man who was bleeding and groaning and moaning from a wound in his lower thigh. He was also now handcuffed. "That's him, Chief Savoie. That's the man who took me out into the alley…that's the man who murdered Wesley," she said, still clinging to Nick.

"Shut up, you bitch," the man said, spitting the words out with rage.

"I'm not going to shut up," she replied angrily. "You killed Wesley, and you drugged me and tried to set me up."

"You were the perfect patsy," he exclaimed with a nasty laugh. "You were as dumb as a box of rocks that night, leaving your drink unattended like you did."

"Did Wesley owe you money? Did he take a bunch of drugs from you and not pay up?" Nick asked.

"Nobody steals from Dax Patrick," he exclaimed fervently. "I don't give a crap if you're some lowlife junkie on the street or some big-ass business man thinking he's smarter than me. Nobody steals from me and gets away with it."

"I've called for an ambulance, and as soon as it arrives, he'll be taken out of here. He'll go directly from the hospital to the jail. We also picked up two men attempting to flee from the scene, and they are also now in custody." Etienne offered Heather a tired smile. "You won't have to worry about this creep or any others ever again. They're all going away for a very long time."

In the light, the evidence of the gun battle was apparent in the holes in the walls. Tearfully, she looked up at Nick. "I'm sorry I shot up your house."

"Oh, honey." He squeezed her tight against him once again. "You can shoot up my house anytime," he said with a gentle smile.

It took another thirty minutes or so for the ambulance to arrive and whisk away the wounded, although the house was still full of police officers.

Heather and Nick had moved into the living room, where they had been questioned by Etienne. "Thank God your security system woke you up," Etienne said. "Otherwise, you would have been shot in bed."

"It did what it was supposed to do," Nick agreed.

They were left alone for a few minutes, and then Etienne approached them again. "I hate to tell you both this, but you're going to have to find other accommodations for the rest of the night. This is now a crime scene, and we'll need to process it and do a full investigation."

Nick frowned and looked at her. "I suppose we can get a room at the motel."

"That isn't necessary," she replied. She took Nick's hand in hers and held his gaze. "Come to my shanty, Nick. We'll be safe there now." There was nothing she would like more than to invite him into her world as he had invited her into his.

An hour and a half later, Heather unlocked the back door to her shanty and they entered. "Wait here," she said, stopping him just inside the door. She went ahead of him and turned on several of the battery-operated lights to illuminate their way through the dark place.

Nick followed her and when he reached the living room, he sank down on her sofa and she sat next to him. "I'm exhausted yet wired at the same time," she said.

He laughed. "I feel the same way. Nothing like a little gunfight in the middle of the night to wake you up."

"I was so terrified, Nick," she confessed.

"Want to know a little secret?" he asked.

"Sure." Her gaze held his.

"I was more than a bit scared myself," he replied. "But in a gun battle, I'd definitely pick you as my partner."

"I never want to be in a gun battle again," she replied.

He released a deep sigh, and they both were quiet for several long moments. "It's nice here," he finally said. "It's so peaceful."

"It is," she agreed. "It's part of what I love so much about it."

"I think I'm ready for some sleep now," he said. "There's at least a couple hours of night left before morning."

"I'm ready for bed, too." She stood and held out her hand to him. He took it and also rose from the sofa. She led him into her bedroom, and she immediately turned on the light next to the bed.

The last time she had been in here, she'd been screaming for her life, hoping somebody, anybody, would come and help her against the three men who had broken in. A cold chill streaked up her back at the memory, but it couldn't persist against the fact that she had survived that night.

They had each packed a hasty bag at Nick's before they left. The bags were left unopened as he stripped down to his boxers and she pulled on a nightgown from her dresser drawer. Then, together, they got into the bed.

He immediately pulled her against him, and she relaxed into his arms. "We made it, Heather," he said sleepily. "The bad guy is in jail, and your innocence has been proven now without a shadow of a doubt."

"All's well that ends well," she replied, even as an overwhelming sadness tugged at her heart. This would probably be the very last time she slept in his arms. There was no more reason for her to stay in his home.

As she listened to his soft, rhythmic breathing mingling with the sound of bullfrogs croaking their nighttime songs, she finally fell asleep.

She awakened before Nick and quietly slid out of bed without waking him. She went into the bathroom to wash her face and then headed for the back porch to start her generator.

The plants in her kitchen looked good and healthy, letting her know that Lucy had taken good care of them while Heather had been gone. She pulled out her coffee maker and got it working and then grabbed from one of the cabinets the two-burner stovetop she cooked on.

This morning, she could cook Nick breakfast because he wouldn't know how things were done in the swamp. She checked her cooler, grateful that somebody had kept ice in it to save the items inside. Thank goodness for good friends, she thought. She was truly blessed in that aspect of her life.

She pulled out a carton of eggs, a package of shredded cheese and a stick of butter. She placed them all on the counter, and by then there was enough coffee to pour herself a cup.

She sank down at the table and sipped the hot brew, her thoughts filled with Nick. She had a feeling that today was going to be goodbye, and her heart already hurt at the very thought.

There was no other reason for her to remain in his home now. She was no longer in danger from anyone and no longer needed his and Bruno's protection.

He would probably take her back to his place to pack up the last of her things and then would bring her back here to begin their lives apart. Her heart squeezed tight, and hot tears pressed at her eyes. She swallowed hard against them. The last thing she wanted was for Nick to see her cry over him. He'd seen her cry over many things already, but she refused to let him see her cry over him.

She'd been a fool to think that a man like Nick could ever really love a woman like her. In the end, she was simply a swamp rat he'd desired but didn't love.

At that moment, he walked into the room. He was dressed in a pair of jeans and a light blue T-shirt. "Good morning," he said with the smile that always warmed her heart.

"Good morning. Sit and I'll pour you a cup of coffee, and breakfast is coming right up," she replied. "Although breakfast won't be as elaborate as what you're used to."

"To be honest, I wasn't expecting anything." He sat at the small table, and she got him a cup of coffee.

"How did you sleep?" she asked and pulled her skillet from a cabinet. She also got out her toaster.

"Like a baby," he replied. "What about you?"

"The same." She stayed focused on making the breakfast of scrambled eggs and toast. She didn't want to look at him for too long because she feared her heart-break would explode right out of her.

As they ate breakfast, they talked about the night that had passed. "I'll be interested to find out who this Dax Patrick really is. I realized after I heard that name that I'd heard it before."

"Oh really, where?" she asked curiously.

"My latest client was involved in a bar fight with him. My client told me at the time that Dax was not from around here and was an outsider. I'd like to know what specifically brought him to Crystal Coves to deal drugs."

"I certainly had never heard of him before. I still don't understand why he used me as a fall guy in the murder," she said.

"I understand why. Like he basically said, you were a woman all alone and vulnerable. The truth is you just happened to be at the wrong place at the wrong time," he replied.

"So, just like you suspected, Wesley was killed over drug money," she said.

"Which just goes to show that dabbling in drugs can be very dangerous," he replied.

They finished breakfast and she cleaned the dishes, insisting his help would be more of a hindrance in the small space.

Once that was finished, Heather returned to the bed-room while Nick sat on the sofa waiting for her. She dressed and then returned to the living room.

"I just spoke to Etienne," he said. "The police stayed all night at my place, and it's now clear for us to return." He stood and at that moment Heather realized she didn't want to go back to his place.

"I'll just stay here," she said. She couldn't go back to the space where she had been so happy with him and not completely lose it. "I grabbed most of my things from there last night. Any clothes I have left there you can donate to a charity."

He looked at her in surprise. "Are you sure?"

She nodded. "I'm positive."

"Then…uh… I guess this is goodbye," he said slowly. He bent down and picked up the small duffel bag he'd brought with him the night before.

"Nick, I'm in love with you." The words blurted out of her. She was unable to hold them in any longer. She needed to say the words to him before he left for good.

He dropped the duffel back to the floor and stared at her. "I'm madly, crazy in love with you," she said and took a step closer to him. "Nick, I don't want this to be goodbye. I want to spend the rest of my life with you. I want to have your babies and build a family with you."

"Heather, I'm sure you're just grateful to me," he finally replied as a deep frown creased his forehead. "Considering everything we've been through, it would be easy to mistake gratitude for love."

"You silly man. Don't tell me how I feel. Of course, I'm grateful to you, but that has nothing to do with the deep love I have for you," she replied.

"I just think you're confused," he said, obviously uneasy.

"Dammit, Nick. I'm not confused," she said with a touch of anger. "I am deeply in love with you."

He stared at her for several long moments. "How can you love me?" he finally said. "I'm unlovable. Delia certainly didn't love me. Hell, my own parents didn't love me enough to stay home from their fancy dinners and jet-setting lifestyle to spend time with me," he said sharply.

It was her turn to stare at him, suddenly seeing the depths of his childhood neglect in the darkness of his eyes. "Oh, Nick, that only speaks to something being wrong with your parents, not anything wrong with you."

She took another step toward him. "You are a kind and caring man. You're intelligent and you have a great sense of humor. What's not to love? And I think if you look deep in your heart, you'll discover that you're in love with me, too." Her heart pounded in her chest, and she felt as if this was the most important moment of her life.

She saw it then…a flash of emotion in his eyes that gave her hope. It was there, love shone bright from his eyes, and then he looked away from her, and when he gazed at her once again, it was gone.

"Heather, you're a beautiful, intelligent woman. Sure, I enjoyed your company. We had a crazy physical attraction to each other. Despite everything that was going on, we had fun together, but I'm not in love with you."

"You're lying," she exclaimed. "You do love me, Nick. Why don't you see that we belong together? I'm not your parents, and I'm definitely not Delia. I'm a woman who will love you with all my heart for the rest of your life."

"I... I don't know what else to say to you."

She studied his features, already memorizing them for when she wouldn't see him again. "What are you so afraid of, Nick?" she finally asked desperately.

"I'm not afraid of anything," he protested and once again averted his gaze from hers. "I'm sorry, Heather, but I'm just not in love with you."

There was nothing left for her to say. Apparently, no words she could speak were going to change his mind. She watched dully as he once again picked up his duffel bag. "I'm sure we'll see each other around town," he said. She followed him into the kitchen and to the back door.

"Goodbye, Heather," he said and then walked out of the back door and out of her life.

She went back into the living room and collapsed on the sofa, unable to hold back her tears any longer. She'd won in that she wouldn't have to stand trial for murder, and she had survived all the attempts to kill her. But she'd lost the most important thing of all... Nick.

"GIRL, YOU NEED to get out of this shanty," Lucy said to Heather almost two weeks later. The two of them sat on Heather's sofa, and another day was slowly coming to an end. Her trial date had come and gone. Etienne had called her to let her know all charges against her had been dropped and that the three men arrested at Nick's house had also been the three who had broken into her shanty.

"I've been busy," Heather protested. "I've had things to do around here."

"Like what?" Lucy challenged her.

"Well, for one thing, I had to get a new front door put on." Heather had hired Brett Mayfield to take care of the job. He was one of the few handymen in town who would come to the swamp to work.

"That was done over a week ago. Why aren't you going into your shop?"

Heather released a deep sigh. "I'm planning on going in tomorrow. I just haven't felt like doing much of anything lately."

"You've got to pull yourself together, Heather. I know that man broke your heart, but you can't let this break your spirit," Lucy said softly.

Heather released another sigh. "I know and I'm going to pull myself together starting tomorrow."

"You swear?" Lucy eyed her dubiously.

Heather laughed. "I swear."

"The town fair is in three days. Are you planning on going?" Lucy asked.

Heather's heart constricted at thoughts of the fair. She had thought she'd be going with Nick, but that certainly wasn't happening now. "I don't know. I would imagine it's not much fun to go by yourself."

"I wish I didn't have a date. I would have much rather gone with you instead of with Arnie Foray."

"Arnie is a very nice guy, and you'll have a good time. I'll just stay home that day and enjoy the solitude," Heather replied.

"That's the problem, Heather. You are getting way too much solitude," Lucy said.

Heather laughed. "I promise that won't be the case

starting tomorrow." Her laughter died, and she stared at her friend. "Can you keep a big secret?"

"You know I can. We've kept each other's secrets safe since we were kids. So, what's the secret?"

Heather swallowed hard. "I... I think I might be pregnant."

Lucy's eyes widened. "Wha...what makes you think that?"

"I'm three days late, and normally I'm never late." Heather reached up and touched the gold necklace she still possessed, then dropped her hand back to her lap.

"How on earth did you allow that to happen?" Lucy asked. "I thought you were on the pill."

"I am." Heather frowned. "You know I was on those heavy antibiotics right before everything happened. And then with everything that was going on, I forgot to take my birth control pills several times."

"Oh, Heather," Lucy replied. "What will you do if you are pregnant?"

"I'm not going to follow in the footsteps of poor Marianne," she said.

For a moment she remained silent as she thought of tragic tale mothers in the swamp used to warn their daughters about sleeping with town men.

She placed a hand on her flat belly. "If I am pregnant..."

"If you are, then are you going to tell him?" Lucy asked.

Heather frowned thoughtfully. "I don't know. I certainly don't expect anything from him. This is my issue, and I haven't thought yet about telling him. Besides, I could be wrong about the whole thing and I'm not pregnant. I might just be late."

"The first thing I'm going to do in the morning is bring you a home pregnancy kit. One way or another, you need to know. I'll make sure you have plenty of time to pee on a stick before we both have to go to work," Lucy said.

LATER THAT NIGHT, Heather was in her bed and thinking of the possibility that she might carry Nick's child. She would never, ever get pregnant on purpose in an attempt to trap him. It was only in the last couple of days she'd thought about how many birth control pills she'd missed over the past couple of weeks. There had been more than several missed pills. She'd been out of her element and not in her normal routine, and that was the only excuse she had for the lapse.

This baby—if he or she truly existed—had been an accident, but Heather would love and nurture it with utter happiness and joy. The baby was wanted, and she would try to be the best mother she could be.

The next morning, true to her word, Lucy was at her door with a bag from the pharmacy in town. "I bought two for you to take. Just to be sure." Heather sat on the sofa next to Lucy as she took them out of the bag, and together they read the instructions.

"Well, they look easy enough," Lucy said. "So go pee, and then we'll wait and see the results."

A few minutes later, Heather came out of the bathroom, the two test sticks in her hands. She set them on the coffee table, and nervously she waited for the results to show.

"Well, congratulations," Lucy said a few minutes later when both tests indicated Heather was, indeed, pregnant. "You know I'll be here to support you through it all," Lucy said.

"I know." Heather reached out and gave her a big hug. "Thank God for good friends."

A thrill rushed through her, followed by a sweet rush of heat. In nine months' time, she would be a mother. The joy was only tempered by the fact that Nick hadn't loved her.

Later that morning, she opened up her shop. She spent part of the morning watering all the plants and the rest of the morning dusting and doing general cleaning.

She was happy when Mrs. Albertson came in. Marigold Albertson was as colorful as her name. The older woman had been a regular customer of Heather's before she'd been charged with murder.

"It's so nice to see you back here where you belong, Heather." She reached up and adjusted the colorful floppy hat she wore on her silver-blue hair. "You have to be glad to have all that nastiness behind you. Of course, I never believed any of it about you."

"Thank you, Mrs. Albertson. I appreciate that."

"And now I would appreciate some fresh parsley and oregano and a bay leaf or two. The weather is cooling off a bit, and so I'm ready to make some of my soups."

"That sounds lovely," Heather replied as she moved to the display that held those herbs.

Minutes later, Marigold went happily on her way,

and Heather sank down on the stool behind the register. Pregnant. She still couldn't believe it. It was a piece of Nick she would always have with her.

She still didn't know if she would tell him or not. On the one hand, she felt like it was none of his business since he'd kicked her to the curb. But the other part of her thought he had a right to know, and he had a choice of whether he wanted to be in the child's life or not.

She didn't know how long she'd been sitting there when she saw him—Nick. He approached her door, and her breath caught in the back of her throat. Had Lucy told him about Heather's pregnancy? No, Lucy wouldn't betray her that way.

He walked into the door. "Good morning, Heather," he said.

She stood from her stool. "Uh…good morning to you," she replied. Oh, why was he here? Just seeing him again stabbed her like a sword into the very center of her heart.

However, he looked like hell. His blue eyes were dull and lines of what appeared to be sheer exhaustion traced down the sides of his face. He was clad in jeans and a gray T-shirt. Still, her heart squeezed tight at the very sight of him.

"It's good to see you back here where you belong. I was wondering when you were going to open your store again."

"Are you here for the plants I owe to you?" she asked, grateful that her voice was calm and even and not displaying any of the emotional turmoil whirling around inside of her.

He shifted from one foot to the other, looking incredibly uncomfortable. "Actually, I'm here to ask you a very important question."

"And what's that?" she asked curiously.

"Have you now realized that what you felt for me was a lot of gratitude and nothing more?" His gaze held hers intently.

"Absolutely not. My love for you hasn't stopped. I'm in love with you, Nick, and it's going to take me a very long time to get over loving you. I'm not sure I ever will get over you, so why are you really here?" This was killing her...seeing him again.

"Because Bruno has told me I've been a miserable bastard without you, and it's true." He took a step toward her. "I've been absolutely miserable without you, Heather. I think about you all the time, and it's an ache in my heart that never, ever goes away."

Her heart began to beat in an accelerated rhythm as she continued to stare at him. What was he saying? What did this mean? He took a step toward her. "Heather, I fought against it, but the truth is I'm madly in love with you. I want to spend the rest of my life with you."

Tears welled up in her eyes. This time they were tears of joy. "Are you sure, Nick?" she asked tremulously. "You have to be very sure."

"I've never been so certain of something in my entire life." He took another step toward her. "But I was so afraid that you'd realize you didn't love me. You were right—I was afraid to take a chance on you."

"You have nothing to be afraid of. I love you, Nick,

and nothing is going to chan…" She didn't get the full sentence out of her mouth before he had her in his arms and his lips took hers in a tender, loving kiss that brought tears to her eyes.

The kiss ended, but he still held her close and gazed deep into her eyes. "I don't have a ring, but, Heather LaCrae, would you be my wife…would you marry me as soon as possible and build a family with me?"

"Yes, oh yes, Nick," she replied, joy exploding through her veins and warming her heart…her very soul. He kissed her once again, and in the kiss, she tasted his unmistakable love.

They finally stepped apart from each other, but he held her hand tightly. "We have a few things to work out," he said.

"Like what?" she looked at him curiously. She was in the very best dream of her life, and nothing he could say would take away her happy glow.

"Like swamp versus town," he replied. "I know you love your shanty. How about we spend weekdays in town so I can work, and then we spend weekends at the shanty?"

"That sounds perfect," she replied. But she had a secret to share with him, and she wasn't sure how he was going to take the news. However, now was the time.

"Nick…when you talked about building a family, how soon did you want that to happen?"

"Whenever you're ready." He gazed at her adoringly. "You've given me back the dream I'd once had of a wife and family, and I'm excited about having both. Why? When do you want to start working on a family?"

Nerves suddenly fluttered through her. "Now," she said. "In fact, we not only already started, but your family is going to increase by one in about nine months."

He looked at her in confusion. Then she saw the exact moment he realized what she'd said.

"You're pregnant?" he asked.

She nodded. His eyes widened, and a huge smile curved his lips. "For real?"

"For real," she replied, a new happiness rushing through her as she saw the shining from his eyes.

"Life doesn't get any better than this. I'm going to be a husband and a father. Heather, I'm so excited about the life we're going to have together. Thank you for loving me," he said humbly.

"Thank you for loving me back," she replied.

He pulled her against him once again. "I got you, Heather. I got us." He kissed her once again, the kiss one of promise. It promised love and laughter and a lifetime of happiness.

ETIENNE SAT NEXT to the hospital bed. It was almost midnight, and the hospital was quiet. He held Colette's slender hand in his and watched her breathe in and out. Over the last couple of months, he'd watched her bruises slowly fade and her skeletal body gain weight.

She was a beautiful woman, and with the medical treatment she'd been receiving, much of her natural beauty had returned. Her cheeks had some color, and her long, dark hair was once again shiny.

"Colette, it's safe now for you to wake up," he said softly. "Nobody is going to hurt you again."

He'd been talking to her for the past hour as he'd done night after night, hoping she would crawl out of the darkness that she clung to. The Swamp Soul Stealer had three women and three men and presumably was holding them someplace deep in the swamp. He would continue to kidnap people from the swamp unless he was stopped.

Etienne hoped like hell that Colette held the key to catching the man. But before she could help, she had to wake up. "Colette, you're safe now. You don't need the darkness anymore. You can come to the light." He squeezed her hand lightly, hoping for any kind of response, but there was none.

He would be back here the next night and the night after and for as long as it took to coax the sleeping beauty awake.

* * * * *